Jacob and the Mandolin Adventure

Jacob
and the
Mandolin
Adventure

ANNE DUBLIN

Second Story Press

Library and Archives Canada Cataloguing in Publication

Title: Jacob and the mandolin adventure / Anne Dublin.
Names: Dublin, Anne, author.
Identifiers: Canadiana (print) 20200333704 | Canadiana (ebook)
20200333712 | ISBN 9781772601626
  (softcover) | ISBN 9781772601633 (EPUB)
Classification: LCC PS8557.U233 J33 2021 | DDC jC813/.6—dc23

Cover illustrations by Talya Baldwin

The author gratefully acknowledges the support of the Ontario Arts
Council. This book is a work of fiction. Names, characters, and incidents
either are the product of the author's imagination or are used fictitiously.

Printed and bound in Canada

*Second Story Press gratefully acknowledges the support of the Ontario Arts
Council and the Canada Council for the Arts for our publishing program.
We acknowledge the financial support of the Government of Canada
through the Canada Book Fund.*

**ONTARIO ARTS COUNCIL
CONSEIL DES ARTS DE L'ONTARIO**

Canada Council   Conseil des Arts
for the Arts   du Canada

Funded by the Government of Canada
Financé par le gouvernement du Canada

 Canada

Published by
Second Story Press
20 Maud Street, Suite 401
Toronto, Ontario, Canada
M5V 2M5
www.secondstorypress.ca

MIX
Paper from
responsible sources
FSC   FSC® C103567

For Meryl

"The sound of the mandolin is a very curious sound because it's cheerful and melancholy at the same time, and I think it comes from that shadow string, the double strings."

—RITA DOVE, U.S. POET LAUREATE

"The Almighty never abandons an orphan. Always He sends a friend."

—LENA KÜCHLER-SILBERMAN, *ONE HUNDRED CHILDREN*

"You shall not wrong a stranger or oppress him, for you were strangers in the land of Egypt. You shall not ill-treat any widow or orphan."

—*EXODUS, 22:20–21*

PART ONE
THE OLD WORLD

On Szmulowizna
the wistful children
chew the moon.

—FAJWEL FITERMAN, "SZMULOWIZNA STREET"
IN *MEZRITSHER YIZKOR BOOK* (TR. BY JERROLD LANDAU)

Chapter 1

Mezritsh, Poland

1927

Jacob hurried along the cobblestone road. He had only a few more blocks to go, but the bag of potatoes he had bought at the market was weighing him down. He had offered to get more potatoes when the cook ran short, but now he wondered if he should have asked someone to come with him.

The loose sole on one of his shoes kept flapping on the stones. The sound was loud in Jacob's ears—over people talking and yelling, wagon wheels squeaking, and horses clopping along the busy road. He walked as quickly as he could and tried to keep his eyes down. He wished he were invisible so that no one would notice him.

His stomach growled. There was never enough food at the orphanage. The members of the orphanage board often had to make appeals in the synagogue or even go knocking on doors for a few more *groshen* for the "poor motherless orphans."

Suddenly, the hulk of a boy stepped into Jacob's path. Jacob's lips trembled and his thin shoulders started to shake. Bartek, the son of the Polish handyman at the orphanage, always seemed to know where Jacob was. He was determined to make Jacob's life a misery.

Bartek flicked Jacob's cap, knocking it off his head and into the mud by the side of the road. "Where are you going, *kijanka*, tadpole?"

Jacob licked his lips. "I'm…I'm going home."

"Home?" Bartek took a step closer to Jacob. His body blocked the hot sun. Jacob would have felt relieved for this respite if he hadn't been so scared. He could smell the bigger boy's sweat and bad breath. He tried not to gag. Once, he had vomited all over Bartek's shoes. Bartek had beat him so hard he couldn't stand up for days.

"You don't have a home." Bartek narrowed his eyes. "You're just a little rat, looking for a hole to hide in." He balled his hands into fists and pounded Jacob on the head as if it were the drum in the klezmer band Jacob had once seen at a wedding. Whose, he couldn't remember. It didn't matter now.

Jacob took a step back, and another, then tripped

and fell down hard on the stones. The bag of potatoes broke, and the potatoes spilled out and rolled away in all directions.

"Even a rat knows how to run better than you do." Bartek scowled. "See you around, little rat." He grabbed a handful of potatoes from the ground, examined one carefully, and hurled it at Jacob's head. Jacob barely had time to duck before the potato hit the wall behind him and lay in a squashed lump on the ground. Bartek scarcely glanced back at Jacob who lay sprawled in the mud.

Jacob scrambled to his feet. He pulled his ragged shirt out of his pants and put as many potatoes as he could into this makeshift pouch.

He hiccupped and, with the back of his hand, wiped the tears that were flowing down his dirty cheeks and the snot from his nose. His elbows were scraped, his cap was filthy, and his pants were torn.

♫

Thoughts kept spinning around Jacob's head as he plodded toward the orphanage. Some of the other children said he wasn't a "real" orphan, but he felt he was—as much as his friends Ezra and David were. They all slept on thin mattresses on similar iron cots, wore the same hand-me-down clothes, and ate the same food day after day—potatoes, beans, and black bread.

It was true that after his mother and father had died, Uncle Isaac and Aunt Malka had taken him in. He was only four years old then and didn't take up much room. He slept on a pallet on the floor in the back room of Uncle Isaac's shoemaker shop. But he grew bigger and their family did, too.

Jacob sighed. Last year, when he was twelve years old, Uncle Isaac had arranged for him to go to the Jewish orphanage.

Jacob had pleaded not to go. "I can help you in the shop. I promise I won't be a burden. I'll even eat less." As if to betray him, his empty stomach had growled.

Uncle Isaac raised his bushy eyebrows and put his arm around Jacob's shoulders. "You are a good boy, but we cannot support you any longer." He blew his nose (honking like a goose) and patted Jacob's head. "Who knows? This might be the beginning of a whole new life for you."

Chapter 2

Jacob finally reached the orphanage, his heart beating so loudly he thought all the children could hear it. The sweat was pouring down his face. It was one of the first warm days of spring. Purple crocuses peeped up from the ground and the song of sparrows filled the air. But the day no longer gave Jacob any pleasure.

He could taste the salt on his dry lips as he wiped his shoes on the mat and entered the wide foyer of the building. It was almost time for the midday meal, but he didn't hurry. He wondered if he would get into trouble for being late or for losing some of the potatoes.

"There you are, Jacob!" He heard Mrs. Anna Adler's voice before he saw her. Her dark brown hair was cut in a short bob and a pair of spectacles hung from a cord around her neck. She wore a dark-colored cotton blouse, a simple, mid-length gray skirt, and sensible black shoes.

Mrs. Adler, or "Anusjka" as she was known to almost everyone in town, walked up to Jacob and frowned. "Jacob, my boy, what happened to you?"

Jacob raised his chin. "I'm…I'm all right." He swallowed hard. "It was Bartek. He…he stopped me in the street."

Mrs. Adler raised her eyebrows. "Again? I will speak to his father!"

"Please don't! It will just make things worse." He kicked the floor with a scuffed shoe. "Sorry, Mrs. Adler."

"There is nothing to be sorry for." Mrs. Adler put her hand gently on Jacob's shoulder. Her touch reminded him of his mother, or how he imagined Mama must have felt like. So long ago. Mama didn't seem real to him anymore. He tried to blink back his tears.

"Hurry along to the kitchen now," Mrs. Adler said. "Give the cook those potatoes and then wash up for dinner." She paused and smiled. "I have an important announcement to make for our children like you, who are over twelve years of age."

♫

The older boys and girls were seated on wooden benches at long tables. Their teachers were seated at the front.

Jacob glanced at his teacher, Chaim Lew. Mr. Lew taught music and led the mandolin orchestra at the school. Jacob thought of his mandolin lessons as he looked at Mr. Lew's long delicate fingers.

When he had first come to the orphanage, he could not play a musical instrument. While he had lived with Uncle Isaac and Aunt Malka, the family would sing *zmiros*, songs after the Sabbath meal was over. From time to time, Jacob would pass by a house and through an open window, he could hear someone practicing violin. His heart yearned to connect to the music drifting out through the air and his fingers ached to play. Why he felt like that, he did not know.

One time, he had even asked his uncle if he could take violin lessons. Uncle Isaac had shaken his head and said, "I'm sorry, my boy. There is no money for you to take music lessons." Uncle Isaac sighed. "Or for any of my children, either." Jacob understood and never asked again.

But when Jacob arrived at the orphanage, everything changed. Every day, the orphans would have their lessons in the regular school subjects—reading and writing Yiddish and Hebrew, mathematics, science, history, and geography. But the children all belonged to the mandolin orchestra as well—no matter what level their skill or how musical they were.

Jacob remembered how he felt when he had first been given a mandolin. How the instrument seemed to fit against his body like a long-lost friend; how his fingers felt awkward at first but then he learned the fingering and the chords. He could now sometimes play without even thinking about what he was doing.

Sometimes when Jacob missed Mama or Papa, he would hold the mandolin against his chest, warming it with his body. The mandolin seemed like something almost alive, with its warm wood and the way the strings vibrated. He would strum the chords and pick at the notes. While he played, he forgot his hunger, his loneliness, his longing for a real home and family.

♫

A stranger was seated at the table next to Mrs. Adler. The man's linen suit was cut differently from the style worn in the town. He held himself in a more confident way than most of the Jewish men Jacob knew.

"Attention, children!" Mrs. Adler rapped on the table. "Quiet please."

The chatter gradually died down as the children turned their heads toward Mrs. Adler. "Children, I'd like to introduce you to our visitor, who has come all the way from Detroit. In America."

Everyone started talking at once.

"Who do you think he is?"

"Why is he here?"

"Where is this Detroit?"

"This gentleman is Mr. Eli Greenblatt," Mrs. Adler said. "He grew up right here in Mezritsh. When he was young like you, he went to America." She smiled and held out her arms. "Listen. He will tell you about an exciting plan he has."

Mr. Greenblatt stood up, wiped his forehead with his handkerchief, folded the cloth carefully, and put it back into his pocket. He cleared his throat, began to speak, and cleared his throat again. "Dear children, I am here to offer you a wonderful opportunity."

Everyone began talking again.

Mrs. Adler raised her hand. "Quiet, children. Please!"

Mr. Greenblatt nodded. "The Mezritsher *landsmanshaft*, our group in Detroit, has heard about this orphanage. We have been working very hard to raise money to bring you children to…America." He sipped some water and put the glass down carefully on the table. "We, who originally came to America from Mezritsh, believe that America is a land of opportunity. A land where you can be whatever you want; if you work hard, you will prosper."

He held out his hands, palms up. "In fact, if I may brag a little, I have done very well for myself in the shoe business." He paused and looked at the faces of the orphans. "The group has sent me here, as its representative, to see if some of you poor orphans would like to go to America." He gazed at Mrs. Adler. "Of course, with permission and visas and so on and so forth."

"I've heard talk about America for years," Ezra said, "but I never thought I might be able to go."

"Imagine me, in America!" Sula said.

"Me too!" Perla said.

"And me!" Rose said.

"When do we go?" Nathan said.

"Soon, I hope," Jacob said.

"But I don't know how to speak English!" David said.

Mr. Greenblatt held up his hands. "Let me explain something. The situation is complicated. As you may know, the doors to America have been shut tight to us Jews since 1924. It has been almost impossible to enter the country."

Mrs. Adler shook her head. "For these past three years, nothing has changed."

Nathan stood up. "So why are you here if we can't go to America?"

"You're just wasting our time!" Abe the Tall said.

"Let's go," Nathan said.

Mr. Greenblatt spread his hands out. "Wait a minute! Please sit down and hear what I have to say."

"Please, boys," Mrs. Adler said.

The two boys shrugged and sat back down.

"We think we have found a way to get around the immigration problems." Mr. Greenblatt shifted back and forth on his feet. "At least, for you."

"How?" Jacob said.

"What does he mean?" Ezra said.

"Wait, boys. I'll tell you," Mr. Greenblatt said. "I've been in touch with a man who owns a large farm in Canada. His name is Morris Saxe. He is a good Jewish man and he has agreed to help you children come to Canada."

"Canada? But that's not America!" Nathan said.

"You're right," Mr. Greenblatt said. "But Canada is close to America." He shrugged. "Maybe one day, when you're grown up, you'll come to Detroit; maybe join the Mezritshers there." He paused. "Anyway, this is a chance for you to leave Mezritsh and make a new life for yourselves." He stared out the window for a moment and then brought his gaze back to the children. "I don't think there's much here for you. Am I right?"

Some of the children nodded; others sat still and seemed unsure how to answer.

Mr. Greenblatt took another sip of water. Jacob could see his Adam's apple going up and down.

"But does Canada allow Jews in?" Mrs. Adler said. "Are not the doors to Canada shut, too?"

"A good question." Mr. Greenblatt nodded. "Yes, the doors to Canada are also closed except—"

"Except?" Mr. Lew said.

"Except for agricultural workers!" Mr. Greenblatt grinned. "You children will learn farm work on Mr. Morris Saxe's farm."

"The girls, too?" Sula asked.

Mr. Greenblatt shook his head. "No. Not the girls. They will be trained to work as domestics."

"What does that mean?" Perla said.

Mr. Greenblatt shrugged. "Cooking, cleaning, sewing...you know, domestic work."

"Like being a servant in a house?" Rose said.

"Yes, but...it will be in Canada," Mr. Greenblatt said. "And from there, who knows?" He snapped his fingers. "From there, when you are older, maybe you will come to America!"

"If they wish to go," Mrs. Adler said.

Mr. Greenblatt shrugged. "Of course."

A stunned silence greeted these words. A moment later, pandemonium broke out in the room.

Chapter 3

"Children," Mrs. Adler said, "*Kinderlech*, please quiet down!" She so seldom raised her voice that the chatter died down almost at once. "Let Mr. Greenblatt explain a few more things to you."

Everyone turned to face the front of the room, although Jacob could still hear muffled whispers here and there.

"There are a few conditions we must follow." Mr. Greenblatt raised his index finger. "One. Only those children who have no mother and no father will be allowed to go." He pursed his lips. "I mean to say, only those children who are full orphans."

Nathan's shoulders fell. "That lets me out. My father is still alive—may he grow like an onion with his head in the ground." He pressed his lips together. "Even though he put me here when I was little. When Mama died."

Jacob put a hand on Nathan's shoulder. "Isn't there a way you can still go?" he whispered.

"Not in a million years!"

Jacob wondered if it was wrong to feel relieved that both his parents were dead. He nudged Ezra. "What about you? Can you go?"

"Of course. Sure. Probably."

"Quiet, children," Mrs. Adler said. "Listen. There's more."

Mr. Greenblatt nodded and held up a second finger. "Two. All children who go to Canada must be in good health. Strong. Ready to work on a farm." He wagged a finger at the children. "It will be a big change for you, city children like you who are not used to hard work on a farm."

He flexed his biceps muscle, trying to look like a muscle builder. He looked so ludicrous—this short, skinny man in his fancy suit—that everyone burst out laughing.

Mr. Greenblatt blushed and joined in the laughter. "But seriously—"

Ezra raised his hand.

"Yes?"

"Will there be horses on the farm?"

Mr. Greenblatt nodded. "Of course, there will. And lots of cows. Mr. Saxe has a creamery in the town where he sells milk, cheese, and butter." He smiled. "And chickens by the thousands!"

"That's for me," Ezra said. "I've always wanted to ride a horse!"

"Feh!" Nathan said. "Smelly chickens!"

"You're just saying that because you can't go," Ezra said.

Nathan glared at him. "Oh, be quiet!"

Jacob could see tears filling Nathan's eyes. He wished he could help his friend but felt helpless. *I'm just a kid who can't change the rules.*

Mr. Greenblatt raised a third finger. "Number three. The children who are chosen must be between thirteen and eighteen years old."

Alex, the youngest child at Jacob's table, groaned. "I'm only twelve." He raised his hand and stood up. "Please, sir, can I go, even though I'm not thirteen yet?"

"I'm sorry, but you can't. I didn't make the rules."

"Don't worry," Jacob patted Alex's back. "Maybe we can find a way."

Mr. Greenblatt frowned in Jacob's direction and raised a fourth finger. "Finally, if you have any close relatives here in Mezritsh—an uncle, an aunt, a grand-parent—we must have written permission from them to allow you to go." He turned to Mrs. Adler. "Your director will contact your relatives, if necessary."

Mr. Greenblatt smiled wanly. "There. I've almost run out of fingers."

"It's a good thing, too!" Ezra yelled.

Everyone began talking at once: comparing, questioning, complaining, wondering who would be allowed to go and who would have to stay.

Mrs. Adler rose from her seat. "Now, children, you must leave it up to me and Mr. Greenblatt to determine if you qualify." She furrowed her forehead. "In a few days, I will post a list outside my office. If you are on the list, you will have an interview with me and Mr. Greenblatt. But if you are not on the list and think you should be, then you must see me as soon as possible."

Jacob poked Alex with his elbow. "See? Maybe you'll still have a chance."

Alex looked up at Jacob and wiped his eyes with his sleeve. "I hope so."

Mrs. Adler's gaze swept over the children. "One last thing: If you are on the list, you should say good-bye to your relatives soon. Our time is short. You will be leaving in three weeks." She smiled. "I will miss many of you, but I sincerely believe this will be a golden opportunity."

Jacob thought of Uncle Isaac and Aunt Malka. *They will want me to go. Won't they? To start a new life? But how will I be able to, if I don't even know English?* His stomach churned. *Do I really want to go? To leave Mezritsh—everyone and everything I have known my whole life?*

He swallowed hard. *Papa, you told me I should be brave. And I'll try.*

♫

A few days later, all the children crowded in front of the list of names posted outside Mrs. Adler's office.

Jacob stayed near the back of the crowd—wanting to know, not wanting to know. His legs were shaking. Finally, he made his way closer to the front. He skimmed the list—up and down, and up again. None of the names on the ELIGIBLE list was his.

"Why aren't you on the list?" Ezra said.

Jacob shrugged, turned away, and hurried down the hall. He wanted to find a dark corner where he could cry out his disappointment. *Or, is it relief? I'm not sure what I feel.*

"Jacob, wait!" Ezra called. "There must be a mistake."

Jacob stopped in his tracks and looked over his shoulder. "I don't think so."

"But why aren't you on the list?"

"I don't know." *Maybe it's for the best*, he thought. *Maybe I shouldn't go but stay here. But I don't* want *to stay in Mezritsh. There's nothing for me here. Maybe in Canada, I can make a new life for myself.*

Ezra grabbed Jacob's arm and pulled him back toward Mrs. Adler's office. "Come on!" he said. "We're going to see Mrs. Adler. Right now."

Jacob pulled away from his friend. "I don't know. Maybe I shouldn't."

Ezra stood in the hallway, his hands on his hips. "Are you *meshugah*? Crazy? This is your big chance to get out of Mezritsh. Are you going to let it slide right through your fingers?"

Jacob pressed his lips together. "All right. Let's go see Mrs. Adler."

Ezra slapped Jacob on the back. "That's more like it!"

♫

Ezra knocked on Mrs. Adler's door.

"Come in!"

When Ezra opened the door, he and Jacob almost bumped into Alex who was coming out. The boy had a huge smile on his face.

"What happened?" Jacob said.

"I'm going to Canada!" Alex spun around on his heels. "I'll turn thirteen before the ship sails, so I get to go." He ran down the hall. "See you later! I've got to tell everyone the good news!"

Mrs. Adler looked up from the papers on her desk and took off her glasses. They swung from the cord around her neck.

She was sitting on a swivel chair behind an old wooden desk with drawers on both sides. All around the room, bookcases were crammed with books. Some were piled on the windowsills and some were even stacked on the floor and looked ready to topple over.

"Yes, boys. What can I do for you?"

Jacob looked down at the worn carpet and tugged on his shirt. "I…I—"

"He wants to know why he's not on the list to go to Canada," Ezra said.

Mrs. Adler looked from Ezra to Jacob. "I see." She put her glasses back on and riffled through the papers on her desk. She took one out from the bottom of the pile. "Jacob, it seems that your uncle did not sign the permission letter."

Jacob took a step forward. "He what?"

"I'm sorry." Mrs. Adler sighed. "Without his permission, we cannot let you go."

"That's not fair!" Ezra said.

"I…I don't understand," Jacob said. "Why didn't he give me permission to go?"

Mrs. Adler stood up and walked around the desk. She put a hand on Jacob's shoulder. "Jacob, I believe you are a good candidate to go to Canada. Would you like to be on the list?"

"I…I think so."

"You *think* so?" Ezra said. "I *know* so!"

"If you can get permission by Monday," Mrs. Adler said, "then I will put you on the list. I promise you."

"Thank you, Mrs. Adler," Jacob said. "I'll do my best."

Mrs. Adler smiled. "That is all anyone can do."

Chapter 4

On the following Saturday, Jacob set out from the orphanage to visit his aunt and uncle. All the children had been obliged to attend the Sabbath service in the morning.

To Jacob, the service seemed to last forever. Thoughts kept running through his head about what he would say, what his aunt and uncle would say, even what his cousins would say. His feet kept tapping; his fingers kept twitching. Several times, the rabbi glared at him and held his finger to his lips.

After the service, he had nibbled the *cholent*, the Sabbath midday meal of beans and vegetables. At last, he was free! He stepped out of the building and took a deep breath.

The rain had cleared the pungent smells wafting

from the tannery and the brush-making factories—smells that sometimes made him feel like choking. People said the work in those factories shortened their lives. *Another reason to leave this city*, Jacob thought.

He made his way along Lubliner Street for a few blocks and crossed the bridge over the Krzna River. The bridge and the adjacent streets were already filling up with people out for a Sabbath stroll and wanting to hear the latest news and gossip.

He soon reached the area where most of the Jews of the town lived—Szmulowizna. It extended through city blocks and alleyways, running every which way, filled with old, crumbling houses lying one on top of the other on top of a swamp. He often wished there were trees and grass on the street.

He finally reached Brisker Street, where Uncle Isaac had his shoemaker shop. The faded sign over the shop had a picture of a pair of shoes. Under the sign, Jacob read the words in Yiddish:

SHICH UND SHTIVEL
NAY UND TSUREKHT MAKHN

SHOES AND BOOTS
NEW & REPAIRED

Jacob walked along the footpath that crossed the drainage ditch. Finally, he reached the low, narrow building.

He peeked through the dusty front window where he saw odd pairs of shoes and boots, packages of faded shoelaces, tins of polish. The display had been the same since Jacob came to live there nine years ago.

He knocked on the front door. No answer. He knocked again more loudly. Finally, Uncle Isaac peeked through a crack in the shade. His face was creased, for he must have just woken up from his Sabbath nap. He had a short black beard peppered with gray. His fingers seemed to be permanently stained from working with leather and polish from sunrise to sunset.

"Jacob, my boy! Come in!" Uncle Isaac opened the door wide and beckoned Jacob to enter. "We were hoping you would come." Jacob followed his uncle through the shop to the kitchen. "We will have tea." He winked. "And maybe a little something sweet."

"Sit down, Jacob. Don't be a stranger!" Uncle Isaac paused. "Too bad the children aren't here. They went for a picnic in the country."

"Oh," Jacob said. "I was hoping to see them, too."

"Don't worry. Another time."

"Maybe."

Uncle Isaac raised his bushy eyebrows. "What do you—?"

Aunt Malka hurried into the kitchen from the back room. "Jacob! What a nice surprise!" When she hugged him, Jacob could feel her bones through her dress. Aunt Malka was as thin as Uncle Isaac was stout. She bustled to the samovar that sat on the counter.

Jacob sat down on the kitchen chair. The table was covered with Aunt Malka's best white Sabbath cloth. On the sideboard, he saw the brass candlestick with dried-up pieces of white wax that had dripped from the night before.

Aunt Malka took the teapot that was resting on top of the samovar, poured a small amount of strong tea into cups, and filled the cups with hot water from the samovar spigot. "Here," she said, placing a cup in front of Jacob. "Drink your tea and tell us all about your plans." She shook her head back and forth and smiled. "Such a big boy. Going to America!"

"Not America, Aunt. Canada."

Aunt Malka shrugged. "America. Canada. What is the difference?" She hit her forehead with her palm. "Oy! I almost forgot the cookies!"

"Sit, Malka," Uncle Isaac said. "I'll get the cookies."

"You shouldn't," Aunt Malka said. "You work from morning to night—"

"Sit, woman," Uncle Isaac said. "What I say, goes."

Aunt Malka smiled. "All right. If you say so."

Uncle Isaac placed a plate of cookies on the table. "Here they are. Your aunt's special cookies. Eat."

Aunt Malka eyed Jacob critically. "You are nothing but skin and bones. Don't they feed you at that orpha… place?"

"Yes, Aunt, but not with such delicious cookies." He took one cookie and nibbled on it. He wished he could take another one, but he knew there was often not enough food for the family.

Aunt Malka beamed.

Uncle Isaac sat down on the chair opposite Jacob. "*Nu*? I am sure you will not get such good cookies in Canada. If you go."

Jacob glanced at his uncle and then looked down at his hands. He could feel his face getting red. "Uncle, why didn't you give me permission to go?"

"Why didn't I?" Uncle Isaac rose to his feet and began to pace the small room. "I'll tell you why."

"What is this about?" Aunt Malka said. "I thought you had signed the paper Mrs. Adler gave you."

Uncle Isaac sat back down and put his head in his hands. "I am so sorry, Jacob. I need to think about this a little more—"

"But why?" Jacob felt the knot in his stomach tighten. "Don't you want me to go?"

Uncle Isaac sighed and picked up his cup. He glanced at Jacob over the rim. "To tell you the truth, I was wondering whether I *should* give you permission. Whether I should let you go so far away."

"To America," Aunt Malka said.

"My dear wife, the boy is going to Canada!"

Jacob could hear water dripping from the faucet. Uncle Isaac put his cup down slowly. "Me, I have never been further than Siedlce, where I went once to sell some shoes and boots." He paused. "I was happy to get home, believe me."

"Isaac, what are you thinking?" Aunt Malka said. "Of course, the boy should go!"

Uncle Isaac drew circles on his plate with a few drops of spilled tea. "It's just…it's just I promised my sister—your mother, may she rest in peace—I would take care of you."

Jacob straightened his back. "Uncle, by letting me go, you *will* be taking care of me." *I hope that what I'm saying is true.*

Uncle Isaac reached out and put a hand on Jacob's shoulder. "All right, my boy. I understand that this is an opportunity that may never come again." He stood up. "Tomorrow, I will go to Mrs. Adler and sign the paper."

Jacob ran over to his uncle. He hugged him tightly, at least as much as he could get his arms around his uncle's stout body. "You will? Really?"

"Yes, my boy. I will." Uncle Isaac unwrapped Jacob's arms and ruffled his hair. "I promise."

"Thank you, Uncle," Jacob said.

Uncle Isaac nodded. "I only hope this is for the best." He swallowed hard. "But I will miss you."

"So will I," Aunt Malka said. "But now tell us all about it."

For the next hour, Jacob related what he knew about the upcoming trip: The orphans would travel by train to Danzig, where they would board a ship called the *Estonia*. The trip across the ocean would take about ten days. They were supposed to land in Halifax, Canada, and then travel by train to Toronto. From there, he wasn't sure how they would get to the farm.

"Across the ocean!" Aunt Malka said.

"So far!" Uncle Isaac shook his head. "One more thing. This man Goldblatt—"

"Greenblatt," Jacob said.

Uncle Isaac shrugged. "Goldblatt. Greenblatt. It does not matter."

"Of course, it matters," Aunt Malka said.

"Greenblatt then," Uncle Isaac said. "It's just a feeling I have. That something is not quite right."

"What do you mean?" Jacob said.

"What is that man getting out of this?" Uncle Isaac said. "I mean, usually a person doesn't do something unless he gets something back."

"Maybe he's doing it because it's a *mitzvah*, a good deed," Aunt Malka said.

"You mean, because the Torah says we should help the widow and the orphan?"

"Exactly."

"I guess the Torah meant someone like me," Jacob said.

"Still, I wonder…," Uncle Isaac said.

Jacob nodded. "I do, too." He took a big breath. "I'd better be getting back now, or Mrs. Adler will worry."

"We'll miss you," Aunt Malka said.

"I'll miss you, too," Jacob said.

Chapter 5

Jacob wiped the tears from his eyes as he opened the door and stepped out into the street. It had started to rain again. As he struggled to do up the buttons of his jacket, he had the uneasy feeling that someone was watching him. He looked up.

Bartek was facing him. His feet were spread on the path over the drainage ditch, his mouth in a sneer. "Where you going, Yid?"

Jacob took a big breath. "Just visiting my uncle." He wished he could dash back into the house or that he could shout for help. But his aunt and uncle had probably gone back to their bedroom and would not hear him. He clenched his fists. *I have to face Bartek on my own.*

He began to edge toward the side of the path. Bartek

seemed to know what Jacob was thinking. He mirrored every one of Jacob's movements. "You don't want to pass, do you?"

Jacob looked down on the ground. "Yes."

"Say please."

"Please."

"Please, sir."

Jacob balled his hands into fists. "Please...sir."

Bartek stepped closer to Jacob, yanked him around, and twisted Jacob's arm behind his back. "Louder!"

Jacob's arm and shoulder were burning like a red-hot iron. He gritted his teeth. "Please, sir!"

Bartek twisted Jacob's arm again but finally let go. He pretended to make a bow and stepped aside. "Since you were so polite."

As Jacob passed in front of him, Bartek shoved him sideways. Jacob lost his footing and, before he knew it, he was lying face down in the muddy ditch.

Bartek kicked some dirt into the ditch. Jacob covered his face with his arm.

"You think you're better than me because you're going to Canada!"

"No...I—"

"Shut up, you stupid Yid!"

Jacob wasn't sure but as he glanced up, he thought he saw Bartek's eyes glistening with tears.

Bartek turned away. As he looked back over his shoulder, he shouted, "I hope the ship sinks!" These were the last words Jacob ever heard Bartek say.

♪

Jacob was busier during the following weeks than he had ever been. Every eligible child was examined by the doctor: height, weight, history of past illnesses. Those who had a heart condition or tuberculosis or walked with a limp were eliminated.

Every morning, the children were woken up earlier than usual in order to do calisthenics to "toughen you up for farm work," Mr. Greenblatt said. They also continued their daily lessons in reading, mathematics, history, and geography.

One day, Jacob overheard Mrs. Adler say to Mr. Lew, "It is important to keep to regular routines as much as possible. We do not want these children turning into *vilde chayas*, wild animals, while they're waiting to leave."

An added urgency hummed in the air now. Mrs. Adler hired a teacher of English and, every day after their regular classes, the "chosen ones" gathered together for an English lesson. They learned how to say, "Good morning" and "How are you?" and "How much do these potatoes (carrots, onions, turnips) cost?"

Of course, the older boys wanted to learn how to say to a girl, "You're very pretty" or "Will you go for a walk with me?" The girls, on the other hand, wanted to say, "Yes. I'll be happy to" or "No. Stop bothering me." Everyone wanted to learn how to say, "Where is the toilet?"

"I wish I could pick up English as fast as you can," Jacob said to Ezra as they were leaving English class one day.

Ezra put his arm around Jacob's shoulder. "It's not so hard."

"Maybe not for you," Jacob said. "I can't get the sound of 'th' like in 'thimble' or 'think.'"

Ezra turned to face Jacob. "Look, all you have to remember is to put your tongue between your teeth and breathe out."

"I'm trying but I don't think I'll ever get it," Jacob said. "My 'th' sounds like 't' no matter how hard I try."

"Yes, you will." Ezra ran ahead. "Come on! We'll be late for orchestra practice."

Three times a week, Jacob hurried to the music room where he and the other members of the mandolin orchestra practiced their music. Jacob remembered how hard it had been at first to play the simplest notes and chords; how his fingers had been too soft and weak, and sometimes even bled. But with time, he had developed calluses on his fingers and some mastery of the instrument.

Uncle Isaac had been true to his word. The day after Jacob had gone to see him, Uncle Isaac had come to the orphanage, spoken to Mrs. Adler, and signed the permission letter to allow Jacob to go to Canada.

Jacob had not slept well since then. His mind felt like a spider's web, filled with all kinds of thoughts that kept him up at night. In the morning, he woke up cranky and bleary-eyed.

It was now two weeks since the list had been posted. On one of their last days of practice, Jacob gathered his courage. "Mr. Lew?"

Mr. Lew looked up from tuning his mandolin. "Yes, Jacob?"

"Sir, may I ask you why you're not coming with us?"

"Yes, sir," Ezra said. "We want you to come, too!"

"Yes! Yes! Yes!" the other children said.

Mr. Lew looked at his students for a moment. He took a clean, pressed handkerchief from his pants pocket, wiped his eyes, and blew his nose. Then he folded the handkerchief carefully and put it back into his pocket.

"My dear students, there is nothing I wish more than to accompany you to that good country of Canada." He shook his head. "Sadly, I cannot."

The students groaned.

Mr. Lew held up his hand. "I have family responsibilities here in Mezritsh. My sick mother…." He pressed his lips together. "I must stay."

Jacob felt an ache in the pit of his stomach. *One more loss. One more good-bye.*

Mr. Lew inhaled deeply and let his breath out slowly. "Another teacher, Mr. Podoliak, will go with you. I am sorry. I cannot go."

"Mr. Podoliak?" Ezra said. "But doesn't he teach the younger kids?"

Mr. Lew nodded. "Yes, but he is an excellent musician and even composes music from time to time."

"He was my first teacher here," Abe the Tall said.

"He's all right," Nathan said.

Mr. Lew riffled through the pages of music on his music stand and smiled at his students. "Now, where were we? Yes. Let's begin at bar eighteen of 'Shulamis in der Wiestenis' by Goldfaden, one of my favorite composers."

He held his hands out, palms up. "Who knows? Perhaps one day, you will play this piece in a famous concert hall!"

Chapter 6

June 1927

The children were allowed one suitcase each. They had been given a list of what to wear or pack:

- Two changes of everyday clothes; one best suit or dress for the Sabbath
- Underwear (3 sets)
- Socks (3 pairs)
- Pajamas (2)
- Jacket or coat
- Cap (for the boys); kerchief or hat (for the girls)
- Handkerchiefs (2)
- Sweater
- Comb, toothbrush, tooth powder
- Towel

Jacob carefully placed each item into his suitcase. *Will I feel different than I do now? Will I feel like a Canadian boy? Will I still feel Jewish?*

He glanced at himself in the mirror that Aunt Malka had given him the last time he visited his aunt and uncle. He made a face in the mirror. He was an ordinary looking boy with brown eyes, curly brown hair, and a round face.

Aunt Malka had hugged him hard until he thought the breath would be knocked out of him. "God be with you, dear nephew."

Uncle Isaac had folded Jacob's hand around a *zloty* bill. "Take care of yourself, and—"

"—Write us a letter from time to time," Aunt Malka said.

"I will." Jacob swallowed hard. "Thank you for everything you've done for me."

Uncle Isaac shrugged. "That is what family is for."

♪

Mr. Greenblatt had told them that, when they arrived in Canada, they would be given the rest of the clothes they would need before the harsh Canadian winter set in.

"What will it be like in Canada?" Ezra said.

"Does it snow a lot?" Jacob said.

Mr. Greenblatt smiled. "You haven't seen a winter like they have in Canada." He raised his arm above his head. "Snowdrifts taller than me!"

"You're kidding!" Jacob said.

"I don't believe it," Ezra said.

Mr. Greenblatt wagged his finger. "Just you wait and see."

On top of his clothes, Jacob gently placed three objects he had kept all these years, the only things he still had left from his family after they died of influenza: Mama's brass sewing thimble, Raisele's homemade rag doll, and Papa's pocket watch. None of these things were valuable to anyone else, but to him, they were priceless.

At times, when he felt lonely, he would put the thimble on his finger and imagine Mama sewing by the kerosene lamp in the kitchen. He remembered how Raisele used to cuddle her doll. She liked to pretend the doll was her baby; she sang songs to her or had a "tea party." Jacob remembered how Papa would wind his watch carefully, seriously, making sure the time on his watch matched the time on the big clock in the Mezritsh town square. *Maybe one day, I'll get Papa's watch fixed. One day when I'm in Canada.*

Jacob sighed as he closed the lid of his suitcase. The lock had broken a long time ago. He fastened the lid with a piece of strong rope and began to fill out the label Mrs. Adler had given to each of the children.

JACOB WEISS, he wrote in his best printing.

Then he added, JEWISH FARM SCHOOL, GEORGETOWN, ONTARIO, CANADA.

It felt strange to be writing in English, but he knew this was a language he must learn, and quickly.

Even stranger was the feeling that he was really and truly leaving. With each step he took, he knew he was moving further and further away from the only place he had ever known. He took a big breath and picked up his suitcase. With one hand, he carried his suitcase and with the other, the case that contained his beloved mandolin.

He was ready. It was time to go.

♪

Mrs. Adler stood in the hallway as the children gathered around her. She raised her hand for quiet. The excited chatter died down almost at once, although here and there, Jacob heard whispers and giggles. One glance from Mrs. Adler made everyone realize this leave-taking was a serious business.

"Children," Mrs. Adler began, "we in Mezritsh have done our best to give you a good home, even though…," her voice seemed to catch, "even though we could never replace your dear departed parents."

"You were wonderful," Sula said.

"I liked it here," Alex said.

Mrs. Adler placed her hand on her chest. Her eyes were shining. "You are all good Jewish boys and girls. I wish you *mazel*, luck, on your way to your new home in Canada." She took a handkerchief out of her pocket and wiped her eyes. "God bless you all!"

"Three cheers for Mrs. Adler!" Ezra yelled.

♪

With everyone's shouts ringing in his ears, Jacob stepped out onto the street and began to walk toward the train station along with the other departing children. As they tramped along the street, Jacob felt a lump in his throat. Never again would he see these people or these buildings or these streets.

Mr. Podoliak walked in front of the group. He pushed his wire-rimmed glasses up to the bridge of his nose; looked behind him to see that everyone was following him; peered at street signs to make sure they were going the right way. *He's like a mother hen with her chicks*, Jacob thought.

A group of old men were sitting on a bench in front of a corner store. They were enjoying the late spring sunshine. Jacob heard one of them say, "They're the lucky ones. Leaving this town and going to America!"

A man with a grizzled beard said, "What are you talking about? Don't you know this is *Gan Eden*, the Garden of Eden?"

The first man glared at him and spit on the ground. "The Garden of Eden, my foot!"

Chapter 7

Mr. Greenblatt was waiting for them at the station. He stood out from the crowd with his straw hat, three-piece linen suit, and light-colored coat. To Jacob, he seemed to exude an air of confidence from the New World— from that almost mythical land called "America."

"I know you're very excited to get on the train," Mr. Greenblatt began, "but before you do, I need to tell you a few things." He held out a large, brown paper bag. "Number one. In my bag here, I have your name tags— each one attached with a string. You must put your tag around your neck and keep it on until you board the ship in Danzig." He smiled a crooked smile. "I don't want anyone getting lost or misplaced on the way."

"Do you suppose there's a Lost and Found for Orphans?" Ezra whispered.

Jacob grimaced. "I hope we won't have to wear these name tags all the way to Canada!"

Ezra elbowed Jacob. "I don't want to be labelled like a piece of luggage."

"Me neither."

Mr. Greenblatt glared at the boys and held up two fingers. "Number two. I know that orphans are always hungry, so you'll get something to eat when we arrive in Warsaw."

Everyone clapped and cheered.

"Will it be kosher?" asked David, who had grown up in an Orthodox home. *Is it his way of trying to remember his family?* Jacob wondered.

"Yes. Will it?" several other children asked.

Mr. Greenblatt pursed his lips. "Of course, it will be kosher! What do you think? I would make you eat *trayfe*, non-kosher food?"

"Just asking," David said.

"What a dope!" Benjamin snatched David's cap off his head and ruffled his hair.

"Give it back!"

Benjamin tossed the cap up in the air, Abe the Tall grabbed it and threw it to Alex, who threw it back to David who caught it and pressed it firmly back onto his head.

Mr. Greenblatt waved for quiet and held up three

fingers. "Number three. I expect your *best* behavior during this trip. No fooling around. No shenanigans. And most of all—"

"No hanky-panky!" Abe the Tall yelled.

Mr. Greenblatt smiled faintly. "I realize that you're all young people." He shrugged. "Maybe you already have a boyfriend or a girlfriend."

"Forget it!" Ezra said.

"Girls! Not on your life!" Jacob said. But he noticed that some of the older orphans glanced at each other or even blushed.

"After all, it is 1927," Mr. Greenblatt continued, "and you've probably heard of the carryings-on of those so-called 'flappers'—"

"I wish I could wear a dress up to my knee," Sula said.

"And silk stockings," Rose said.

"And a long pearl necklace," Perla said.

Mr. Greenblatt stared at the girls. "Do I make myself clear?"

"Yes, Mr. Greenblatt!" all the children said (except for Abe the Tall).

Mr. Greenblatt nodded. "All right then." He reached into the bag and pulled out a name tag. "When I call your name, come get your name tag and line up in front of Mr. Podoliak."

Soon, all the children were lined up, their suitcases and instrument cases in their hands. They followed Mr. Greenblatt and Mr. Podoliak onto the platform of the Mezritsh station.

Mr. Greenblatt peered at his pocket watch. "Our train is almost here," he said. "Can you hear it?"

With a grinding of wheels, hissing of steam, and gray smoke staining the clear blue sky, a train rushed onto the tracks beside the station. Jacob had read about trains and heard people talking about them. But now, standing next to the train and getting ready to board, he felt dwarfed by this machine that loomed above his head and blocked out the sun.

♫

Jacob swallowed hard. It took all his courage to put his foot on the two steps up to the train.

He could scarcely see from one end of the car to the other, for the older boys and girls were still standing up. He knew everyone there, as if they were part of a large family: Sula and Alex, Abe the Tall and Faige, David and Benjamin, Perla and Rose. He especially knew the ones his age or who were in the mandolin orchestra.

He then had a thought that made him smile. He

imagined the seats were like frets going across his mandolin and the aisle was like the strings.

"Hurry up, Jacob!" Ezra pushed him from behind. "Stop dreaming and grab a seat. I'll sit beside you."

The two friends plopped down next to each other on seats near the front. Their compartment was filled with the nervous chatter of thirty-eight young people—laughing, teasing, waving at relatives or friends who had come to see them off.

Jacob stared out the grimy window. *Where are Uncle Isaac and Aunt Malka? Couldn't they even come to say good-bye? Maybe they don't care about me like they said they do.* Jacob felt the tears coming to his eyes, but he wiped them away with his sleeve.

Out of the corner of his eye, he saw his aunt and uncle rushing toward their car as the train began to move out of the station. He stood up and opened his window.

"Good-bye, my boy!" Uncle Isaac shouted.

"Take good care of yourself!" Aunt Malka yelled.

"I will! I will!" Jacob said.

The high-pitched whistle blew; the train rounded a bend; the platform was gone. They were on their way.

Jacob took a deep breath and let it out slowly. He sat back down and closed his eyes. *Will I find a new home in Canada?*

Chapter 8

As Jacob stared out the window of the train, he could see the smokestacks of the brush-making factories black against the early morning sky.

Even though he had been very young, he still remembered how Papa used to make brushes. On a table set against the long wall of the kitchen, Papa would first sort the pig hairs and then comb them with an iron comb dipped in kerosene. He would do the work standing up, by the feeble light of the lamp. Jacob remembered clouds of dust that hung in the air over the work. Papa was always coughing; the combined smell of pig hair and kerosene was nauseating. Mama often sent Jacob outside to play.

That memory was still strong, but others were fading into a gray mist as the years passed. Jacob clenched his fists. *I will never forget Mama and Papa and Raisele! Never!*

He smiled to himself. He would also never forget the muddy streets of Mezritsh, or the hunger gnawing in his belly, or the lurking danger of Bartek—always following him like an evil shadow.

Sula interrupted his thoughts. "Does anyone have a bag?" she said. "Alex is going to be sick!"

Jacob turned around to face Sula and Alex. "Are you all right?"

Alex shook his head. His face was pale and almost green.

Sula said, "No one is paying any attention to me."

Jacob nodded and stood up. He held tightly to the back of the seat in front of him. "Hey, everybody!" He waved his arms. "Quiet down, everyone!"

"What do you want, small fry?" David said.

"What's up?" Benjamin said.

Jacob pointed to Alex. The boy was scrunched down in his seat; his hands over his mouth. "Alex is feeling sick. Looks like he's going to throw up."

"Yuck!" Perla held her nose.

"Ugh!" Rose said.

The two girls did everything together, as if they were twins. But Rose had blond hair and blue eyes while Perla had dark brown hair and hazel eyes. They both devoured every magazine about Hollywood movie stars they could get their hands on. They tried to look like their idols, Clara Bow and Mary Pickford. They couldn't stop telling people that Mary Pickford had been born in Toronto, close to Georgetown where they were going.

"Please!" Jacob said. "Does anyone have a paper bag? Or something?"

The children started rummaging around in their belongings.

"Hey!" David said. "Let him use his shoe!"

"His hand!" Benjamin said.

"His pockets!" Perla and Rose said.

"Very funny!" Jacob said. "Come on, everyone. Alex needs help!"

Someone passed a newspaper down the rows. Jacob handed it to Sula.

Sula looked at the paper. "I don't know how to fold it."

"Let me do it." Ezra grabbed the paper and quickly folded it into the shape of a cone. He handed it to Sula. "Here you are."

Sula blushed. "Thank you."

"I used to sail paper boats on the river." Ezra looked down at his feet. "You know, before the...orphanage."

Sula nodded and turned to Alex. "Take this."

Alex put his face close to the cone. Jacob thought it

made him look as if he had a long, pointed nose, like the story of Pinocchio he had read in the orphanage library.

Jacob settled back on his seat. "I wonder what he'll be like on the ship," he said. "In fact, I wonder what we'll *all* be like."

Ezra sighed. "I guess we'll soon find out."

♫

The muddy streets and dirty brick buildings of Mezritsh gradually gave way to greening fields of vegetables: radishes, carrots, cabbages, beans, and onions. Jacob's mouth watered to think of the autumn harvest to come.

The apple trees were in full blossom and everywhere Jacob looked, the country was fresh and green. Early June. Jacob had always loved this time of year—a season filled with promise and hope.

The train wheels were humming; the train was swaying. Jacob's eyelids felt heavy. He leaned back in his seat.

He dreamed Mama was sewing a new summer dress for Raisele. His sister kept buzzing about Mama like a pesky fly, asking, "Is it ready yet, Mama? Is it?"

Mama kept shaking her head, while her foot pressed the pedal of the sewing machine up and down, up and down. The flowered cotton moved under her fingers, as if it had no end. "Soon," Mama said. "Soon, my dear." The needle broke; Mama stopped sewing; the machine was silent.

Raisele began to wail. "Now it will *never* be finished! Never be finished! Never be finished!"

Jacob woke up with a start. He opened his eyes. The train whistle was shrill in his ears. Where were they? He looked out the grimy window and saw small houses and gardens that gave way to brick factories belching smoke. They were approaching the city of Warsaw.

Chapter 9

With a great grinding of brakes, the train shuddered to a stop. The orphans stood up, stretched, and started to gather their belongings together. They pushed and shoved, talked and laughed as they moved down the corridor toward the door.

Mr. Greenblatt stood at the front of the car and waved his arms for quiet. He straightened his hat and tightened his tie. He cleared his throat and began to speak. "Children, we've just finished the first part of our journey. As you must realize, we have a long way to go."

Jacob's stomach was churning. He felt like throwing up. He shook his head, took a big breath, and straightened his back. *This is a great adventure. I have to be brave, just like the explorers who sailed around the world a long time ago. And maybe, just maybe, I'll find a real home at the end of this journey.*

Everyone began talking at once, but Mr. Greenblatt held up his hand. "I know you're anxious to leave the train, to stretch your legs, to eat something—"

"Maybe a sandwich?" David said.

"I'd like a nice piece of *vursht*, salami, on rye bread," Benjamin said.

"With a pickle," Abe the Tall said.

Jacob could see Alex glancing at the older boys. His face still looked rather green.

"All in good time," Mr. Greenblatt said. "Be sure you're wearing your name tag—"

"Right here, Mr. Greenblatt!" Benjamin said.

Mr. Greenblatt furrowed his brow. "Whatever you do, do *not* leave the station." He wagged his finger. "I don't want to look for any lost children."

"Not a chance!" Abe the Tall said.

"We're going to Canada," Benjamin said. "And I can't wait."

Mr. Greenblatt took his watch out of his vest pocket and peered at the time. "It's 11.45 a.m." He snapped the case shut and put the watch back. "The train to Danzig leaves in two hours. Watch your step as you leave the car. Make sure you have everything. And whatever you do, stay in the station."

He hit his forehead with the palm of his hand. "Wait a minute! I almost forgot." He leaned over the seats and peered out the window. "I arranged for the orchestra to play a few musical pieces for the committee from the Warsaw Jewish community—"

"Really?" Ezra said.

"Do we have to?" Perla and Rose said together.

Mr. Podoliak took his place beside Mr. Greenblatt. "Yes. You do," he said. "It will be good practice to play in front of these people."

I hope we play some easy pieces, Jacob thought. *I hope it's over quickly.*

"Yes," Mr. Greenblatt said, "and it's good publicity, too. Maybe we can raise some money to help with our expenses. And after you play—"

"What?" Abe the Tall said.

"You'll get your photos taken with the committee."

The children groaned.

"But I'm starving!" Benjamin said.

"Me too," Abe the Tall said.

"I'm sorry, but I promised." Mr. Greenblatt waved at someone on the platform. "There they are."

"I wish we could eat first, then play and get our pictures taken afterwards," Ezra said.

"I don't even *want* to get my picture taken!" David said.

Benjamin slapped him on the back. "What? Not for posterity?"

"What does that mean?"

Benjamin shrugged. "Forget it. I'll tell you later."

"I guess we'd better do what Mr. Greenblatt tells us." Sula frowned. "But Alex, don't eat too much or too fast. I don't think this traveling on moving vehicles agrees with you."

Alex nodded and looked down at his shoes.

"When we're in the station," Jacob said, "you'd better look for some paper bags."

"Lots of them," Ezra said.

There was a general buzzing of talk as the girls took combs and mirrors out of their purses and combed their hair. A few of the older girls even applied rouge and lipstick, although they knew that Mrs. Adler had disapproved of makeup.

Even some of the older boys quickly ran a comb (or their fingers) through their hair. Everyone grabbed their belongings and descended from the train as quickly as they could.

♫

The railway station was a swirling mass of noise, confusion, and smells—passengers descending from the train and onto the platform; friends or relatives shouting greetings; porters wheeling or carrying cases, bags, and boxes; children running around; babies crying; women sobbing or yelling; men laughing or shouting. The smells of cheese and sausages, pickles and sauerkraut from baskets and bags filled the air.

A small group of men and women were waiting to meet the orphans. They crowded around Mr. Greenblatt. Everyone started speaking at once.

Mr. Greenblatt held up his hands. "Please, ladies and gentlemen," he said. "The orchestra will play a few short pieces for you. Afterwards, we'll have photos taken, and I will answer all your questions."

He gestured toward the station. "If you will kindly follow me...."

Mr. Podoliak pointed to a relatively clear space in the station. "Children, put your suitcases in a pile over there, and get your mandolins ready." He brushed the hair out of his eyes. "We will play only three of the songs we've been practicing." He closed his eyes and then opened them. "'Tum Balalaika,' 'Oyfn Pripetchik,' and 'Zay Meer Gezunt.'" He smiled. "The sooner we finish, the sooner we all can eat!"

"Well, if you put it like that!" Abe the Tall said.

Jacob felt as if all the oxygen had been drained out of the air. His stomach was in a knot and his head was pounding. *Why am I always so nervous before I have to play?* He opened the case, took out his mandolin, and began to tune it.

"Don't worry," Ezra whispered. "You'll be fine once you start playing."

"It's just the part before I play that's always so hard for me," Jacob said.

"But when you play, you forget all that. Don't you?"

Jacob could only nod.

While the orchestra was getting ready, a newspaper reporter rushed over to Mr. Greenblatt. He held a pad of paper in one hand and a pencil in the other. He wore a tweed woolen cap on his head, wire-rimmed glasses, and had a thin moustache above his upper lip.

"Are you Mr. Greenblatt?" the reporter said.

"Yes, and you are?"

The man tipped his cap. "Shmuel Yatskan, from the *Haynt*, the *Today* paper." He licked the tip of his pencil. "We heard you're taking forty orphans to Canada. Is that true?"

Mr. Greenblatt shook his head. "Not forty. Thirty-eight."

"Right. And where are they going exactly?"

"To a farm. Near Georgetown, Canada."

"Georgetown?" Shmuel furrowed his brow. "Where is that exactly? And how do you spell it?"

"Georgetown is near Toronto, a very big city in Canada." He tapped his foot impatiently and looked over Shmuel's shoulder at the people waiting for him. "G-E-O-R-G-E-T-O-W-N."

"I see," Shmuel said. "But tell me, Mr. Greenblatt, I thought Canada wasn't allowing any Jews in. So how did you get visas for all these children?"

Mr. Greenblatt shrugged. "Why do you ask? We got them fair and square."

"But how?"

"These orphans will be trained as farmers or servants in homes. Canada still needs those kinds of workers." Mr. Greenblatt started to move away. "So, we got permission from the government."

"But—"

Mr. Greenblatt pushed past Shmuel. "If you'll excuse me, it's time for the orchestra to play."

"But Mr. Greenblatt, I have a few more questions. Please—"

Mr. Greenblatt shook his head. "I am sorry. I have to go." He turned on his heels and hurried away.

♫

The players bowed; the concert was over; the people in the station applauded. The musicians put their instruments away. When he heard the click of the clasp on his mandolin case, Jacob felt that he could breathe normally again.

"You see?" Ezra slapped him on the back. "That wasn't so bad. Was it?"

"No. Not so bad." Jacob paused. "In fact, once I got over my stage fright, it felt good."

"I knew you'd be fine," Ezra said. "Now let's get our photos taken and then we can eat."

"Good idea!"

Various people from the Warsaw Jewish community gave some speeches, and then the orphans posed for photos.

Finally, they were allowed to line up for lunch. A few ladies stood behind a long table. Everyone got a bowl of steaming cabbage soup, two slices of black bread with butter, a piece of cheese, and an apple.

"This is much better than a sandwich," Ezra said.

"That's for sure!" Jacob said.

Everyone sat down wherever they could. David recited the blessing over the food. For the next few minutes, all that could be heard was the slurping of soup, the chewing of bread, and the crunching of apples, along with several satisfied burps.

Chapter 10

The orphans stood on the platform and waited for the train to Danzig. Jacob gazed down the tracks. They seemed to stretch out forever into the distance.

Why did I want to go so far away? he wondered. *To the other side of the world.* He pressed his lips together. *To find a real home, that's why.* He straightened his back. *Stop being such a baby. Remember what Papa said when he was dying.*

"The world is full of tsuris, *troubles, but you are a good boy. You must face life's challenges with courage and hope."*

I will, Papa. At least, I'll try.

He turned to Ezra and tapped him on the shoulder. "What do you think it will be like?"

Ezra was leaning against a wall and reading a

newspaper that someone had left behind. "What will *what* be like?"

Jacob swallowed hard. "I mean, when we get to Canada."

Ezra shrugged. "It's got to be better than the orphanage."

When they finally boarded the train and found their seats, Jacob sighed with relief. The orphans had the compartment all to themselves. Jacob felt it was a little like being back together at the orphanage. As the train pulled out of the station, he smiled.

"What are you smiling about?" Ezra said.

"I just had a crazy thought."

"What is it?" Ezra nudged him with his elbow. "I'm used to your crazy thoughts!"

Jacob gazed off into the distance. "Just imagine! Maybe ten years from now, when I've made my fortune in Canada, I'll come back here."

"Where is here?"

"Here. To Warsaw. And then I'll go to Mezritsh."

"And what will you do there, oh wealthy man?"

"I'll give *kopecks* and *zlotys* to every beggar I see in the street."

"If you do that, then you'll end up poor, just like them!"

Jacob sighed. "In Mezritsh, I'll see Mrs. Adler and the other orphans. I'll give them money for food and clothes." He held out his hands. "And maybe enough money to replace the leaking roof."

"You know what, Jacob?"

"What?"

"You're full of dreams!"

"I guess I am."

♪

Jacob spent the next few hours chatting with Ezra and Benjamin, reading Ezra's newspaper, and playing a game of checkers that Abe the Tall had brought along.

After he had enough of playing and reading, he stared out the window and watched as the train sped past patches of farmland or clumps of birch or willow trees.

Some of the older kids took out their mandolins and began to play tunes they knew, like "Oyfn Pripetchik" and "Everybody Loves My Baby," a popular English song.

Jacob must have dozed off. Before he knew it, the shrill whistle of the train warned everyone that they were approaching the port city of Danzig.

Jacob was amazed that Mr. Greenblatt's suit still

had a freshly pressed look. He wiped his brow with his immaculate handkerchief. "Hurry along, children!" he said. "Gather your belongings together and let's get off the train." He made a sweeping gesture. "But whatever you do, stay together!"

Gulls squawked and swooped above their heads as the orphans trudged from the train station toward the harbor. The gulls were fighting over a piece of bread that someone had dropped on the road.

Jacob inhaled the cool salt air. He heard the shouts of porters, the cries of fishmongers trying to sell the last of the day's catch, the creaking of ropes and chains, the clanging of bells. The setting sun sparkled on the dark waves and shone on the ships and boats anchored in the harbor or beside the docks.

Jacob gazed at the ship they were about to board. He looked from one end to the other, from bottom to top. He felt very small as he stared up the side of the ship. The ship's masts seemed to prop up the sky; the funnels, to soar upward into the heavens.

At the border station, Mr. Greenblatt undid the clasps of his briefcase, rummaged inside, and pulled out a sheaf of papers. He handed the papers to the heavy-set man in the booth.

"When I call your name, walk over here in front of me," the man said. When he had finished his inspection, he handed the papers back to Mr. Greenblatt and waved him away. "Everything is in order. You may go."

As they walked through the gate, Jacob heard the man mutter, "Good. Thirty-eight fewer Yids in Poland."

"What did that man say?" Benjamin said.

Abe the Tall clenched his fists. "I feel like going back and giving him a piece of my mind. Or maybe my fist."

Mr. Greenblatt prodded the boys forward. "Please. Just ignore him."

"We don't want any trouble," Mr. Podoliak said.

Jacob gritted his teeth. He felt like shouting, "Good riddance to you, and to Poland, too!" But he knew he had to keep silent.

♪

A man in a blue uniform and peaked cap stood at the foot of the gangplank. He had a trim, graying beard and piercing blue eyes surrounded by fine wrinkles. "My name is Mr. Hansen," the man began in heavily accented Polish. "I am the chief steward."

"Pleased to meet you," Mr. Greenblatt said as he shook the steward's hand.

Will I be able to be so confident when I grow up? Jacob wondered.

Mr. Greenblatt handed the papers to Mr. Hansen.

"These are the orphans from Mezritsh. We are ready to board your ship."

Mr. Hansen licked his index finger and counted the papers. "Thirty-eight plus two adults?"

"Yes, sir," Mr. Greenblatt said.

Mr. Hansen surveyed the group. "Let me make something clear." Jacob had the feeling that this man would brook no nonsense.

An orange tabby cat was rubbing its body against Mr. Hansen's legs. It stopped, licked its fur, and gazed at the group of orphans as if saying, "Don't worry. This is a good ship."

"The *Estonia* holds eight hundred passengers," Mr. Hansen said. "You must stay in your section, the 'tourist' section, where everything will be provided for you and—"

"Please, sir," Benjamin said. "How long will it take to get to Canada?"

"We will stop in Copenhagen first," Mr. Hansen said, "but with fair weather, we should arrive in Halifax in less than two weeks."

Alex was looking pale.

"Don't worry." Sula put an arm around his shoulders. "It will pass in a flash."

"I hope so!" Alex said.

"I thought we were going to Canada," Ezra said.

"Halifax *is* in Canada." Under his breath, Mr. Hansen said, "Children nowadays do not learn geography!" In a louder voice, he said, "Halifax is the port where we stop to let you off. Then the *Estonia* will go to New York City, our final destination."

He bent down to pick up the cat. "In case you are wondering, this cat, who is making a nuisance of herself, is our ship's cat." Mr. Hansen stroked the cat's fur. "We call her 'Estie.' She is not a pet for you to play with, for she has an important job to do on the ship."

"I can imagine what it is," Ezra whispered.

"Me too," Jacob said.

"What?" David said.

"Catching mice," Ezra said.

"Mice?" Perla and Rose squealed.

"Do not worry," Mr. Hansen said. "Estie keeps them under control." He gestured behind him. "Now, I will take your tickets and show you to your cabins. We are scheduled to leave in the morning."

As Jacob gave Mr. Hansen his ticket and walked up the gangplank, his heart was racing and his legs were shaking. He was crossing a bridge from the Old World to the New; from his old life to a new one. And he was more scared than he had ever been in his life.

PART TWO
BETWEEN TWO WORLDS

"YAM LID / THE SONG OF THE SEA"

Kh'hob fargesn ale libste,
Kh'hob farlozt mayn eygn hoyz;
Kh'hob dem yam zikh opgegebn.

I forgot my loved ones and
left behind my own home.
I have surrendered to the sea.

—FROM *YAM LIDER/SEA SONGS*
BY CHAIM NACHMAN BIALIK

Chapter 11

Ezra shook Jacob's arm. "Are you still feeling seasick?"

Jacob groaned. "Leave me alone. I think I'm going to—" He leaned over his bunk and threw up in the basin that had been his constant companion during the last two days.

"I'm getting out of here!" Ezra pinched his nose. "I'm sorry I was ever put in the same cabin with you!" With a loud shuffling of feet and slamming of the door, Ezra left the cabin. But then he poked his head back in. "I didn't mean it, you know."

"I know," Jacob croaked.

"See you later!"

Jacob had never felt so sick in his life. At first, when he had stepped onto the wooden deck of the ship, he hadn't noticed the swaying motion. He ate a late supper of bread, cheese, herring, pickles, and fruit. Afterwards, even though Mr. Greenblatt had told the orphans to go to their cabins, he and Ezra had sneaked away to stand on the rear deck.

Jacob gazed at the harbor. "Have you ever seen so many lights?"

Ezra shook his head. "Never."

"I feel so small…so insignificant."

"Me too."

They leaned on the railing and let the night breeze cool their faces. They took turns yelling, "Good-bye, Danzig!" or "Good-bye, Mezritsh!" or even "Good-bye, Poland!"

But in the morning, as the *Estonia* made its way through the choppy waters of the North Sea, Jacob felt nauseous and headachy. Finally, he went to lie down on his bunk—grateful it was the lower one.

For two days and nights, he had been too sick to get up, except to go to the toilet. He dozed fitfully all through that time, scarcely aware of Ezra, who seemed immune to seasickness and kept running up and down the corridor, knocking on doors and yelling, "Are you alive in there?"

Jacob closed his eyes. He imagined the ship was the rocking chair where Mama had held him, and later, Raisele, whenever they needed comforting.

One day, some Christian boys had thrown stones at Jacob on the way from *cheder*, religious school. Jacob had been four years old and almost too big to be rocked, but he had climbed onto Mama's lap, and she had sung the song that still lay snug in his heart:

Shluf mine faygele, Sleep my little bird,
Mach tzu dine aygele, Shut your little eyes,
Eye-lu-lu-lu; Eye-lu-lu-lu.
Shluf geshmok mine kind, Sleep soundly, my child,
Shluf un zay gezunt, Sleep and be well.
Eye-lu-lu-lu. Eye-lu-lu-lu.

Was it magic? Was it wishful thinking? When he woke up, he no longer felt seasick. And he was ravenous!

♫

Singly, by pairs, and then in larger groups, like mice out of their holes, the orphans crept out of their cabins and into the dining room. It was a plainly furnished room with white painted walls, long tables, and benches on both sides. The pipes had been left exposed and the electric lights were simple fixtures attached to the ceiling.

At the first meal, a few kids like David, who wanted to keep kosher, said, "You didn't say we'd have to eat *trayfe*, non-kosher food, on the ship!" He pushed his plate of bacon and eggs away.

Mr. Greenblatt held his hands up. "Don't worry. I'll speak to Mr. Hansen right away."

"I wish I'd never come," David said.

"You can't eat only bread, butter, and herring for the next ten days!" Benjamin said.

"Just watch me!"

"I don't know what you're complaining about," Ezra said as he shovelled a forkful of potatoes into his mouth. "I can't remember when I've had so much to eat."

It turned out that David didn't have to eat only bread and butter for the rest of the voyage. Their group was soon given an ample supply of eggs, fish, and cheese to satisfy even his strict Orthodox upbringing.

♫

On the third day, Mr. Podoliak handed out a timetable to the orphans.

"I don't know why we have to do calisthenics first thing in the morning," Benjamin said.

"Don't you want to be in good shape when we get to the farm school?" Jacob said.

Benjamin grimaced. "Right. Farm school. Horses and chickens. Lots of manure."

"I'm glad we're learning more English here," David said.

Benjamin shrugged. "I guess that'll be useful for something."

"My favorite time is free time," Abe the Tall said.

"Right," David said. "Because you're always looking for someone to beat at checkers."

Abe the Tall grinned and shrugged.

"My favorite time is breakfast, lunch, and supper," Ezra said. "Jacob, what about you?"

"I guess it's mandolin practice." Jacob could almost feel his fingers tingling. "There's something about it that's hard to explain," he said. "It's like I forget about everything else when I'm playing."

The boys were silent for a moment.

"I think I know what you mean," Ezra said.

♪

On the fifth day of their voyage, Mr. Podoliak stood in front of the mandolin players and rapped his baton on the music stand. "Children, I have an important announcement to make."

Everyone looked up from their music.

Mr. Podoliak cleared his throat. "Mr. Hansen has asked us to play a little concert for the passengers in first class." He straightened his back. "He thought the other passengers would enjoy hearing you play."

All the kids started to talk at once.

"Where?"

"When?"

"What do we play?"

Mr. Podoliak rapped his baton again. He handed out a sheet of paper to each player. "I'll answer all your questions tomorrow. Look at this list carefully and put your music in order for tomorrow's practice."

He took off his glasses, wiped them with his handkerchief, and placed them carefully back on his nose. He made a sweeping gesture at the group and smiled. "You've worked very hard. I believe the first-class passengers will enjoy our concert."

He paused. "You may leave early to get your music organized."

The children cheered.

"And maybe practice for an hour on your own?"

The children sighed.

As everyone was leaving, Ezra slapped Jacob on the back. "That will be fun—playing for all those hoity-toities in first class!"

Jacob's back was turned away from his friend as he placed his mandolin in its case. "I...I don't know," he said. "I've never played in front of such grand people before." He snapped the case shut and looked down at the ground. "I don't know if I'm good enough."

Ezra put an arm around Jacob's shoulders. "What are you talking about? You're one of the best players we have!"

"But—"

"No buts! You'll be fine," Ezra said. "Anyway, I can't wait to see what the first-class section is like."

Jacob swallowed hard. "I'm going to look for a quiet place to practice. I need all the help I can get."

Chapter 12

Jacob looked everywhere for a place to practice. He wanted to find a spot where no one would hear him. First, he tried playing in his cabin, but people banged on the walls and told him to be quiet.

Next, he tried the third-class smoking room, but it was filled with men (and a few women). Besides, the smoke and closed air made his throat burn and his eyes water.

The third-class lounge was no better. People were busy reading, chatting, or playing cards. Stewards bustled about, giving the passengers drinks like soda water, tea, or coffee along with cucumber, cheese, or ham sandwiches. Jacob grabbed two cheese sandwiches from one of the trays. As he walked along, he chewed one sandwich and put the other one in his pocket for later.

He peeked into the third-class dining room, empty now except for stewards setting the tables for the evening meal. Near the rear door that led to the dining room, Jacob found a set of stairs he hadn't noticed before. He walked down to the deck below, and then to the one below that.

The air smelled dank and musty. He heard sounds of machinery clanging, of gears and wheels grinding, of turbines turning. He thought he could even hear the propellers churning on the other side of the ship's hull. He stopped on the stairs and tried to decide where to go next.

"Boy, what are you doing here?" a burly man said as he hurried up the stairs.

"I…I'm lost."

The man put a heavy hand on Jacob's shoulder. "You'd better get yourself out of here right now." He pushed Jacob roughly up the stairs. "Passengers aren't allowed down here."

"Yes, sir." At the top of the first flight of stairs, Jacob noticed a door with the sign BATHROOM. Now he was grateful he had learned some English.

He pointed to the door. "Please, sir. I need the… toilet." He swallowed hard. "I have to go bad."

"All right. But be quick about it, and then get upstairs."

"I will."

As the man moved away, he said, "I've had a long watch. No time for lost boys."

When the man was out of sight, Jacob hurried back down the stairs and made his way along a narrow, dimly lit passageway. He saw a sign that said BAGGAGE ROOM, tested the door, and strangely, found it unlocked.

He groped for the switch and turned on the light. One bare lightbulb lit the long, cavernous room. Trunks and boxes of all shapes and sizes reached almost to the ceiling. In one corner, Jacob saw a pile of large canvas duffel bags and decided that these would make a good place to sit and practice.

As he made his way toward the bags, Estie the cat scurried past his feet and out the door. Jacob plopped down on one of the bags and began to tune his mandolin when he felt the bag under him move. His mandolin thrummed in protest as it dropped onto the floor. With trembling hands, he picked it up, grabbed the case, and started to back toward the door. His legs were shaking and his heart was pounding. *Did a snake or some wild animal get into the bag? Maybe it will jump out and attack me!*

Just then, a head with matted brown hair popped out of the bag. A pair of green eyes blinked at Jacob and someone whispered, "Jacob? Is that you?" The boy rubbed his eyes. "What are you doing here?"

"I…I…." Jacob inhaled sharply. "Nathan, what are *you* doing here?"

♪

Nathan crawled out of the bag while he kept his eyes on Jacob. His face was red and his forehead was beaded with sweat. When he had completely slithered out, he dusted himself off and sat down on a box nearby.

"What are you doing here?" Jacob repeated. "I thought you weren't on the eligible list because…your father is still alive. How did you get on the train? And… onto the ship?"

Nathan sighed. "Sit down. It's a long story."

Jacob thought he heard footsteps above him and a faint scratching sound in a far corner. Then he noticed a smell coming from Nathan's body. Jacob pinched his nose with his fingers. "Why does it reek in here?"

Nathan looked down. "I…I didn't exactly have a place to wash."

Jacob released his nose and nodded. "I understand. But really. What happened?"

"Yeah, well. I went to my father and told him I wanted to go to Canada." Nathan hung his head. "He laughed at me. Then he slapped me and knocked me around a bit. Said he was going to take me out of the orphanage. To help him with the business."

Jacob pressed his lips together. "What's his business?"

"You don't want to know."

"I do."

Nathan balled his hands into fists. "All right. I'll tell you. Smuggler. Blackmailer. Robber." He sighed. "That's when I decided that, if I couldn't go to Canada legally, I'd find a way to go illegally." Nathan straightened his back. "So, I did."

"But—"

Nathan shrugged. "Look, I'm not proud of it, but I stole some money from my father, went on the trains with you—in a different compartment so you wouldn't see me—and followed you to Danzig."

"But, Nathan," Jacob said. "Mr. Greenblatt said that only full orphans are allowed to go with him to Canada."

Nathan looked down at the ground. "I know." He licked his dry lips. "But I thought he might make an exception for me. Or—"

"What?"

Nathan looked at Jacob. "I'll lie. I'll tell him my father is dead." He swallowed hard. "He might as well be."

Jacob nodded slowly. "But what about a visa?"

"Look, Jacob. I don't have all the answers. All I know

is that I had to leave Mezritsh." Nathan raised his head and looked at Jacob. He had tears in his eyes. "I couldn't stay there any longer. I wanted to start a new life."

"I know. Me too," Jacob said. "But how did you get on the ship?"

Nathan stood up and began to pace the narrow pathway between boxes and trunks. He winced with every step he took.

"What's wrong with you?" Jacob said. "Why are you limping?"

"Nothing." Nathan sat down again. "All right. I'll tell you." He inhaled and let his breath out slowly. "The night before the ship was supposed to leave, I pulled myself over the wall next to the pier, crept up the gangway, and found this room.

"That's when this happened." He unlaced his shoe, pulled off his sock, and showed Jacob the bottom of his foot. It was red and full of pus. "When I jumped down off the wall, I landed on a nail sticking up from a board." He shook his head. "It went right through the sole of my shoe and into my foot." He rolled his eyes. "You know how thin our soles are. Right?"

Jacob nodded.

"I tried to keep it clean, but this isn't exactly a first-class hotel."

"But—"

Nathan began to put his sock back on. "It's all right. As long as I stay hidden, I'll survive…if I'm lucky." He placed the shoe on the floor beside the duffel bag. He looked at Jacob. "That's about all."

"You've been here for five days? All alone?"

Nathan nodded. "And I'll stay here until we reach Canada." He glanced toward the door. "You'd better go now. A steward checks this room once a day and I think it's almost time for him to come."

Jacob stood up. "All right. Can I come back tomorrow?"

Nathan grinned. "Sure. It's nice to see a friendly face."

Just as Jacob reached for the doorknob, he felt in his pocket and held out the squished sandwich. "Are you hungry?"

Chapter 13

It took a long time for Jacob to fall asleep that night. His head was buzzing with questions. Should he tell Mr. Greenblatt about Nathan? Should he stand by and do nothing? But if he helped Nathan, would he get into trouble, too? And if he didn't help, what would happen to Nathan?

When early morning light began to seep into the small porthole of their cabin, Jacob finally fell asleep.

Ezra was shaking his shoulder. "Wake up, Jacob!" Water from his wet hair dripped onto Jacob's face. "You were sleeping so soundly I thought you'd *never* wake up!"

Jacob turned to face the wall and groaned.

"Come on, Jacob. Get up!"

Jacob turned over, rubbed his eyes, and sat up. "I'll have to keep my eyes open with toothpicks today."

Ezra was rummaging around in his pile of dirty clothes on the floor. He pulled out a shirt, smelled it, and shook it out. "This is clean enough, I guess."

Jacob yawned and stood up. "Ow!" He bumped his head on the bottom of the upper bunk. Again. "What time is it?"

"Eight-thirty. And you'd better hurry if you want any breakfast."

"I'll be there as soon as I can." As he washed his face and brushed his teeth, he kept thinking about Nathan and what he had to do. At breakfast, he stuffed an extra piece of rye bread into one of his pants pockets and a banana in the other.

"You know, Jacob," Mr. Podoliak said in a low voice, "there's plenty of food here. You don't need to take anything extra."

Jacob looked down at his bowl of porridge. He could feel his face growing red. "Sorry. I guess it's an old habit. You know, from the orphanage."

"Well, we're going to a new world. Maybe it's time to get new habits."

As Jacob nodded, he wished he could put more food into his pockets for Nathan. Maybe ten bowls of porridge and an entire loaf of warm bread.

♪

The morning's lessons seemed endless to Jacob.

"Jacob, are you with us this morning?" Mr. Podoliak said.

Jacob's head snapped up. "Yes, sir."

"Well, make sure your brain is here as well as your body."

"Yes, sir."

When the lessons were finally over, Jacob grabbed his books and dashed out of the room.

"Wait for me!" Ezra said. "Where are you going?"

"I...I...have to do something," Jacob said. "I'll see you at lunch."

"But—"

"Sorry!"

Jacob raced along one corridor, through the dining room, down one flight of stairs, but tripped and almost toppled down the second flight of stairs. He held onto the railing to get his balance.

Then, he heard some voices coming up the stairs.

"He thought he could get away with it," a deep man's voice said.

"Not on this ship," a higher voice said. "The captain runs a tight ship."

Jacob's heart thudded in his chest. *Are they talking about Nathan? Did they find him?*

The voices were coming closer. Jacob dashed back up the stairs and hid around a corner. He pressed himself against the wall and tried to make himself invisible. He could almost feel the heat of the ship's engines seeping through the walls.

"Anyone who drinks on duty deserves what he gets," the first man said.

Jacob slowly let out his breath. The voices grew fainter as the men walked away.

"Yeah. Three days in the brig is too good for him," the second man said. "I mean, even if Polish vodka *is* the best in the world."

"You're right. Anyway, we'd better get moving."

"I know. We still have some work to do before our watch is over."

When Jacob was sure the men had left, he walked back down both flights of stairs. He turned the doorknob and opened the door to the baggage room. "Nathan? Are you here? I brought you something to eat."

There was no answer.

Jacob turned on the light and moved closer to the pile of bags at the back of the room. "Nathan?" He heard a muffled groan. He stepped toward the duffel bag where Nathan was hiding. He stooped down, loosened the top, and slid it down to Nathan's shoulders.

His friend's hair was stuck to his head, his face was red and sweating, and his eyes had a glassy look to them.

Nathan licked his dry lips. "Jacob," he croaked. "Is that you?"

Chapter 14

"Of course, it's me," Jacob said. "Who else would it be?"

Nathan groaned and fell back onto the duffel bag. "Do you…have…water?"

"Sorry. I forgot." Jacob stood up. "I'll…I'll be right back." He hurried out of the room, dashed up the stairs, and headed toward the dining room. At the entrance, he skidded to a stop. He wasn't allowed in there until the lunch whistle was blown. He bit his lip, trying to decide what to do next.

Who were the adults he could call upon? Mr. Greenblatt, who had stayed in his cabin since they had boarded six days ago—maybe still seasick? Mr. Podoliak, who seemed to sway with every breeze? Mr. Hansen, who would probably haul Nathan to the captain? And then what? Would the captain put Nathan in the brig for the rest of the voyage? Would he send Nathan back to Poland?

Jacob inhaled deeply, pushed his shoulders back, and slipped into the dining room. First things first. He would find a cup or glass and fill it with drinking water. He would then look for an infirmary or a nursing station, wherever it was, and get some medicine for Nathan. After that, who knew?

He glanced at the stewards in their spotless white jackets as they set the tables for lunch. He could smell onions frying and hoped the chef was preparing *blini* stuffed with cheese and smothered with sour cream. His mouth watered as he thought of the delicious food.

Jacob shook his head. He had to focus on the task at hand. He crept into the room and grabbed a glass from a wide shelf stacked with glasses and cups. Just as he was leaving the room, someone grabbed him by the back of his shirt collar.

"Boy," said a deep voice. "What are you doing here?"

Jacob struggled to free himself from the man's grasp, but it felt like an iron vise. He turned around and peered at the man who belonged to the voice. It was one of the stewards.

The man glanced up at the clock on the wall. "Lunch will be served in half an hour. You should not be here now."

"I...I...need a glass for my cabin."

"For your cabin?" The man looked Jacob up and down. "You one of the orphans?"

Jacob nodded. "Sometimes, I wake up in the middle of the night. I get thirsty."

The man loosened his hold on Jacob and stroked his beard. "My boy also." He pushed Jacob gently out the door. "Take the glass to your cabin, but do not let the chief steward see you."

"Yes, sir. I mean, no sir." Jacob scurried out the door and was about to go down the stairs, but he hesitated. He did not want to go back to the stuffy, dank baggage room. Not yet. He climbed up the stairs—one flight, then another, and still another—until he reached the sun deck. A few passengers were walking back and forth or leaning against the railing.

Estie was playing with the rope of the ship's bell. It made a vague, echoing sound that seemed to reach deep inside Jacob. He felt a yearning for something. What it was, he could not name.

Jacob found a spot where he hoped he wouldn't be noticed. He felt the spray on his face and breathed in the fresh air. The sun sparkled on the waves and a light breeze ruffled the canvas deck chairs and cooled his sweating face. *I wish I could forget all about Nathan and stay up here, where the air is clear and all my worries vanish, way beyond the horizon.*

Jacob straightened his back. *I can't abandon Nathan. Orphans have to stick together. I'll bring water to Nathan, and then follow through with the second part of my plan.* He clenched his fists. *At least, I'll try.*

♫

Jacob dragged his feet down the stairs. He dreaded what he might find in the baggage room. *Maybe I've been exaggerating all of this. Maybe Nathan will be all right by now.* But in his heart of hearts, Jacob knew this was only wishful thinking.

He opened the door to the baggage room. He glanced behind him. Why had he never noticed before how it squeaked on its hinges?

He walked toward the lump in the duffel bag. "Nathan? It's me. Jacob."

Nothing stirred.

"I...I've come back...like I said." Jacob held out the glass of water. "I brought some water."

Nathan's head poked out of the top. He grimaced, trying to shape his mouth into words. He reached for the glass with stiff fingers. "Wa...water," he whispered. "Give me."

Jacob could scarcely make out the words that Nathan uttered. He stooped down and helped Nathan sit up and hold the glass.

Nathan opened his mouth but he could not swallow. The water spilled onto his hands and down his shirt. He began to cough and his body began to twitch. "Can't… can't…stop."

Jacob helped Nathan lie back down and rose to his feet. "I'll get some help," he said. "Don't worry."

"No," Nathan gasped. "Will…send me…back."

Backing out the door, Jacob ran up the stairs. His heart was beating against his chest as quickly as his fingers played the tremolo on the mandolin.

Mandolin! What am I going to do about the concert? Jacob shook his head. *No. My friend has to come first.*

Just as Jacob reached the top of the stairs and turned a corner, he bumped into Ezra.

"Where have you been?" Ezra said. "I've been looking everywhere for you!" His eyes shone. "I've been exploring the ship. You should see what I found!"

Jacob looked down at his shoes. "Uh…I've been… practicing."

Ezra raised his eyebrows. "Really? Then where's your mandolin?"

Jacob could feel his face growing red. "I…I left it somewhere."

Ezra grabbed Jacob's arm and pulled him aside. "Listen, Jacob, if you don't want to tell me, it's okay. Only don't lie to me."

Jacob let out a huge breath. "I'll tell you, but you have to promise not to tell anyone."

"I promise. Now what's this all about?"

Jacob told Ezra that Nathan had stowed away on the ship, that he was very sick, and Jacob needed to find some medicine.

Ezra whistled under his breath. "Gosh! What a pickle!" He paused. "But I'm just the fellow who can help."

"What do you mean?"

Ezra beckoned to Jacob. "Follow me, my friend. I know the very place you're looking for."

Chapter 15

Ezra raced along the corridor with Jacob following closely behind him. Up flights of stairs, along corridors, down more stairs. Jacob felt like a mouse trying to find his way out of a maze.

Ezra skidded to a stop and Jacob bumped into him. Both boys were panting; the sweat poured down their faces.

"Why did you stop?" Jacob said.

Ezra bent forward and placed his hands on his knees. "Stitch in...my side. Got to...catch my breath."

"How do you know where to go?"

Ezra straightened up slowly. "I 'found' a deck plan of the ship."

"What do you mean you 'found' it?"

Ezra peered at Jacob. "You remember when Mr. Hansen told us not to go into the first-class section?"

"I do. And?"

"I asked him to explain where it was," Ezra said. "I told him I wouldn't know where not to go if I didn't have a plan of the ship."

"Good thinking. What did he say?"

"At first, he said that the sections were clearly marked with signs." Ezra grinned. "Then I told him how I've been fascinated by ships since I was a little kid and would he *please* give me a plan of the ship."

"So he did?"

"He did."

Jacob glanced around. "We'd better get moving. If we don't show up for lunch, Mr. Podoliak will want to know where we've been. And I don't want to lie to him."

Ezra licked his lips. "Lunch! I'm so hungry, I could eat a bear!"

"And maybe some blini, delicious pancakes!" Jacob's stomach growled. "Lead on, Ezra. How much farther is it?"

"Not far now. They *would* put the infirmary on the opposite end of the ship from our section!"

The boys hurried up and down more staircases and along corridors, until at last they reached a white door with a painted red cross and the sign, INFIRMARY.

Jacob knocked on the door. No answer. He knocked again. He heard shuffling footsteps coming to the door. A heavy-set man with a balding head and dark eyes opened the door. The man was wiping crumbs from his mouth. The buttons of his white jacket looked about to burst, for his jacket scarcely contained the man's ample stomach. He wore a small name tag that said DOCTOR NOWAK.

"Yes?" Dr. Nowak said. "What can I do for you?"

"I…I…," Jacob began.

Ezra pushed Jacob forward. "My friend here has a headache. He needs some Aspirin."

Dr. Nowak raised his eyebrows. "I do not give medicine to children without the permission of their parents. Besides, Aspirin upsets the stomach, you know."

Jacob put his hand to his forehead. "Please, sir, Doctor, it's only an Aspirin and we've come all the way from the other end of the ship."

"Third-class passenger, are you?" said Dr. Nowak.

"Yes," Ezra said. "We're two of the orphans going to Canada."

Dr. Nowak frowned. "I don't know…. It's against the rules, you know. And if the captain ever found out—"

"He won't!" Jacob said.

Ezra made a motion across his lips. "My lips are sealed!"

Dr. Nowak brushed a few more crumbs from his jacket. "Doesn't the man in charge of your group… doesn't he have an Aspirin?"

"He doesn't," Jacob said.

"He forgot," Ezra said.

"Please, Doctor!" Jacob said. "It feels as if a freight train is running through my head."

"Well, maybe just this once," Dr. Nowak said. He turned his back on the boys and walked to a medicine cabinet at the other end of the room. He unlocked the cabinet, took out a bottle of Aspirin, walked back to the boys, and shook a tablet into Jacob's hand.

"Please, Doctor, may I have one more," Jacob said. "For later?"

"I don't usually do this, you know." Dr. Nowak shook out one more pill. "Wait a minute. I'll get you a glass of water."

"It's all right." Jacob backed away. "I've got some water in my cabin."

"But—"

"Thank you, Doctor." Jacob pushed Ezra out of the room and into the corridor. When they were safely out of earshot, he whispered, "Let's get this Aspirin into Nathan."

Ezra nodded and the boys raced back to the other end of the ship.

♫

Now it was Jacob's turn to lead and Ezra's to follow. He felt the pills in his hand. They were slowly turning to mush in his sweaty palm. He put them into his pocket and retraced their steps—first class, tourist class, third class, dining room—down two flights of stairs until they were standing outside the baggage room.

"I'll go in first," Jacob said. "I don't want Nathan to be startled." He put his hand on Ezra's shoulder. "Give me a minute and then come in."

"Okay."

As Jacob made his way to the back of the room, he could smell something like rotting garbage that had stayed out too long in the hot sun. When he reached Nathan at last, he could barely see the rise and fall of the bag in which Nathan was hiding.

"Nathan?"

All he heard was a groan.

"It's me. Jacob." He undid the top of the bag but the smell made Jacob gag. He backed away, held his breath, and then stepped forward again. He stooped down and tried to help Nathan sit up, but Nathan flopped down as if he were a rag doll.

Jacob groped in his pocket and took out an

Aspirin—along with a few pieces of lint, a rubber band, and a piece of old chewing gum.

"Please, Nathan, take this pill and you'll feel better."

But Nathan shook his head, fell back to the floor, and began to shake uncontrollably.

Jacob pressed his lips together. *Nathan can no more swallow an Aspirin than I can swallow an elephant.*

He rested on his haunches, his elbows on his knees, his head in his hands.

"Jacob?" Ezra said as he came up behind him. "How's Nathan?"

Jacob stood up. "Nathan is so sick that a whole bottle of Aspirin won't help him."

Chapter 16

Jacob and Ezra rushed up the stairs to the dining room. Everyone was already seated at their tables—talking, laughing, eating borscht. Blini were piled high on a platter in the middle of the table, surrounded by bowls of fried onions and sour cream.

"I love blini!" Benjamin said.

"We're lucky the cook made them especially for us!" Sula said.

Abe the Tall helped himself to another serving. "Maybe he's taking pity on us poor orphans."

"For once, I'm not going to worry about my figure," Perla said.

"Me neither," Rose said.

Mr. Podoliak was seated at the end of a table. He was

deep in conversation with one of the stewards. "What would you suggest?" he said. "The veal or the fish?"

The steward leaned forward, making sure his linen towel rested firmly on his arm. "I think the gentleman would prefer the fish."

"I'll—"

Jacob and Ezra hurried to Mr. Podoliak's side. "Mr. Podoliak!" Jacob said. "You have to come quickly!"

Mr. Podoliak pushed his glasses up the bridge of his nose and stared at Jacob. "What is so urgent? Can't this wait until after lunch?"

"No, sir. It can't!"

"It's an emergency!" Ezra said.

Mr. Podoliak peered at the two boys, a slight smile on his lips. "It must be a real emergency if you boys are prepared to skip lunch."

"It is!" Jacob said.

"Please hurry, Mr. Podoliak!"

Mr. Podoliak wiped his mouth with his napkin and stood up. He glanced at his empty plate, the clean knife and fork sitting beside it. "But what is the problem?"

Jacob pulled on Mr. Podoliak's sleeve. "Please come. I'll tell you on the way."

"Where are you going?" Sula asked.

"What's wrong?" David said.

"Don't you want to eat?" Benjamin said.

Ezra eyed the food, but Jacob pulled him away as they rushed out of the dining room with Mr. Podoliak.

After they entered the baggage room, events happened in a flurry of activity. When Mr. Podoliak saw the condition Nathan was in, he hurried to tell Mr. Greenblatt, who rose from his seasick bed and asked a steward to call Mr. Hansen at once. When Mr. Hansen took in the situation, he called Dr. Nowak to come with two strong porters and a stretcher. They carried Nathan to the infirmary, followed by a group of orphans who, by that time, were buzzing with the news of a stowaway on board.

♬

The next morning at breakfast, Mr. Hansen tapped Jacob on the shoulder. "Jacob, you must come with me," he said. "The captain wishes to speak to you in his cabin."

Mr. Podoliak stood up. "I'll go with Jacob."

Mr. Greenblatt held his hand up. "No. I will go with the boy," he said. "I am responsible for all the orphans." His face was pale but he was freshly shaved. His shirt was clean, his suit pressed, but he did not walk with his usual confident step as he and Jacob followed Mr. Hansen along the corridor.

"Are you all right, Mr. Greenblatt?" Jacob asked.

Mr. Greenblatt put his hand on Jacob's shoulder. "That seasickness knocked me for a loop," he said. "But I'll be fine now. Feeling better every day."

Good, Jacob thought. *I need all the help I can get.*

Mr. Hansen knocked on the heavy wooden door of the captain's cabin.

"Yes?" the captain said. "Come in." He was seated behind his desk. He riffled through some papers, picked up a sheet of paper and examined it carefully. He turned to Mr. Greenblatt. "This Nathan…Rosenberg. I see his name is not here."

"No, sir," said Mr. Greenblatt. "I brought only the children who have visas for Canada."

Estie the cat padded around the cabin. Her tail was swishing and her eyes were aglow.

Jacob glanced at the teak-lined walls, the bookshelf crammed with books, the table on which several maps were laid out, the rubber plant that stood on the floor like a sentinel. He wanted to look at anything but at the captain.

"Jacob Weiss, is it?" the captain said.

Jacob nodded.

"Jacob, I want an explanation, and I want it quick," the captain said. "Am I to understand that you *knew* about the stowaway?" He lowered his voice. "That, in fact, you *helped* him?"

Mr. Greenblatt stepped forward. "Jacob is only—"

The captain made a dismissive gesture toward Mr. Greenblatt. "I want to hear what the boy has to say, in his own words."

Mr. Greenblatt sighed and put his hand on Jacob's shoulder. "Tell him, Jacob."

Jacob hung his head and stared at the polished wood floor.

"Speak up, boy!" Mr. Hansen said.

Jacob felt his face growing red. He suddenly had the urge to pee. "I…I only found Nathan two days ago and—"

"Why didn't you report him right away?" the captain said.

"I…I don't know." Jacob pressed his legs together. I…I just wanted to help my friend."

"He's just a boy," Mr. Greenblatt said. "He didn't know what to do."

The captain folded his arms and glared at Mr. Greenblatt. "I'd like to hear the rest of the story from the boy himself, if you don't mind."

Mr. Greenblatt seemed deflated, like a balloon that had lost its air. *He can't help me*, Jacob thought. *I have to do this myself.*

The captain turned toward Jacob. "I understand Nathan comes from the same orphanage you do."

Jacob nodded. "But he wasn't allowed to come with us."

The captain raised his eyebrows. "Why not?"

Jacob swallowed hard. "His father…wouldn't give him permission…to go."

"Speak up, boy!"

Jacob raised his voice. "He…he has a father. And—"

"What?"

"Only full orphans, with no mother or father, were allowed to go."

The captain sighed. "I see. That leaves me few alternatives," he said. "If Nathan survives, and I believe that is highly unlikely—"

"He won't?" Jacob said.

"*Sha*, Jacob!" Mr. Greenblatt said.

The captain held up his hand. "Dr. Nowak tells me it will take weeks for Nathan to recover his health, if he ever does.

"Meanwhile, I will have to make arrangements for his hospitalization when we land in Halifax in a few days' time. If he recovers, he will eventually have to go back to Poland." The captain paused and narrowed his eyes. "At great expense to the Baltic American Line, I may add. Unless…."

"Unless?" Mr. Greenblatt said.

"Unless you can get a visa for the boy."

Mr. Greenblatt shook his head. "I'll try. But I doubt it."

The captain nodded. "I'll check with Dr. Nowak and keep you informed of Nathan's condition. As for you, contact me if you can manage to get a visa for him."

Mr. Greenblatt bowed. "Thank you, Captain. I will."

"May we visit him, sir?" Jacob said.

The captain furrowed his brow. "That will be up to Dr. Nowak."

With these words, Jacob and Mr. Greenblatt were ushered out of the captain's cabin.

Chapter 17

The night after Nathan was moved to the infirmary, Jacob dreamed he saw his mother, her soft brown eyes and gentle smile beckoning him to come closer.

"Is it you, Mama?"

His mother did not say a word.

Jacob took one step toward her, then another, then still one more.

Mama held out her arms to Jacob. Her touch was like the fluttering of a butterfly on his cheek. Slowly, Mama enfolded him in the cocoon of her arms. But soon she began to fade away, like wisps of fog in the sunlight. As she disappeared, she said, "Never forget us."

Jacob woke up. Mama was gone.

He scrambled out of bed. The cabin was filled with dim shadows and the half-light of early dawn.

He reached under the bunk bed and groped for his suitcase.

Quietly, so as not to awaken Ezra, he pulled the suitcase out, untied the rope, and opened the lid. He searched in the satin pocket on the inside of the lid, found the brown envelope, and undid the flap. He stood up and walked toward the porthole.

From the envelope, he pulled out a small black and white photo. Papa stood behind Mama, his hand resting on her shoulder. Both of them were dressed in their best clothes. They stared at the camera, eyes wide open and hopeful. They looked so young!

He pulled out another photo—this one of Mama and Papa looking a little older, with Jacob held between them. How old had he been then? Six weeks? Three months? He couldn't tell. He turned the photo over. Of course, he knew there was no date, but he always searched for one.

A sob caught in his throat. Mama and Papa didn't seem real to him anymore. His memories of them were fading like these yellowing photos. Mama and Papa were buried in the Jewish cemetery in Mezritsh. Would he ever go back there to lay a stone on their graves?

And now, Nathan was so sick, he might die, too. *Should I have told Mr. Greenblatt or Mr. Podoliak about Nathan?* Jacob wondered. *Should I have gone for help earlier? Looked for a doctor?* He felt as if he were choking with guilt.

Jacob brushed the tears from his eyes with his pajama sleeve, put the photos back in the envelope, the envelope back into the suitcase, closed the lid, and shoved the suitcase back under the bed.

He glanced at Ezra, who was snoring softly on the upper bunk. He picked up his mandolin and he began to pluck the strings, picking out the melody of songs the orchestra had been practicing. He hummed softly to himself. *What is it about the mandolin that makes me want to smile and cry at the same time?*

Ezra sat up and yawned. "Why are you up so early? And what are you playing?"

Jacob placed the mandolin in its case. "I couldn't sleep."

Ezra stretched. "Me, I slept like a log!" He climbed down from his bunk and walked toward the door. "Why don't we early birds get ready? Then we can go visit Nathan before breakfast."

"Good idea."

The boys washed, got dressed, and hurried along what were now familiar corridors until they reached the infirmary. When they pushed the door open, they saw Dr. Nowak seated at his desk, his head in his hands and a scowl on his face.

"Dr. Nowak?" Jacob said.

"Yes?"

"Can we visit Nathan now?"

"Your friend the stowaway?"

Both boys nodded.

Dr. Nowak sighed. "I'm sorry but you can't visit Nathan. He is a very sick boy. High fever. He can't talk."

"Will he...get better?" Jacob said.

"He has to!" Ezra said.

Dr. Nowak inhaled deeply and let his breath out slowly. "I do not know. Only time will tell." He gazed into the distance. "If only...if only there was a way to cure these terrible infections...."

He banged his fist on the desk. "Right now, all we can do is hope that time, and perhaps God—your god or mine—will heal your friend."

Jacob's stomach churned. "Isn't there...something... anything we can do?"

"We want to do something!" Ezra said.

Dr. Nowak brought his eyebrows together. "Pray, boys. Pray."

"It's all my fault," Jacob muttered. "I should have told you sooner."

"There is no cure for tetanus, you know," Dr. Nowak said. "Nothing you could have done would have made a difference once the infection took hold."

He shook his head, as if trying to clear his thoughts. "I heard that you orphans are giving a concert tomorrow night for the first-class passengers and senior crew. I hope to attend."

He stood up. "Now I must see to your sick friend."

"Thank you, Doctor," Jacob said. "We'll come again tomorrow."

♪

At breakfast, Mr. Podoliak said, "Because of the concert tomorrow night, we must have an extra practice today."

"Oh no!" Abe the Tall said. "I want to play ping-pong."

"Me too," Benjamin said.

"I want to finish my book," Rose said.

"And I found a new magazine I want to read," Perla said.

Mr. Podoliak wagged his finger at the mandolin players. "No excuses. No tardiness." His shoulders sagged. "With all the trouble and worry about Nathan, you haven't been applying yourselves. We have no time to waste."

"But sir," Ezra said. "What will happen to Nathan? Will he be allowed to stay in Canada?"

"If he gets better…," Jacob said.

"I don't know," Mr. Podoliak said. "Mr. Greenblatt has been sending cables to Halifax, to Ottawa, and even to Mr. Morris Saxe at the farm school. Mr. Greenblatt is trying to get a visa for Nathan."

"He has to!" Jacob said.

"We can't worry about that right now." Mr. Podoliak looked at the clock on the wall. "I too am concerned about Nathan, but we must rehearse for the concert. And I mean today!"

"This ship is like a prison," Abe the Tall said.

"What were you expecting?" David said.

"A pleasure cruise maybe?" Benjamin said.

Chapter 18

Jacob was so nervous, he thought he would throw up. The good thing was that while the orchestra had been rehearsing these past two days, he could forget his worries about Nathan for a few minutes at a time. The bad thing was that Mr. Podoliak had given him his first solo, "Oyfn Pripetchik." And he was terrified.

He had practiced until his fingers were numb. He had practiced until his back ached. He had practiced until his head felt as if it were stuffed with *matzah brie*, fried matzah.

All that practicing didn't seem to help. *Breathe*, he said to himself. *Relax*. But all he could do was picture himself in front of the first-class passengers, dressed in their fancy clothes and sparkling jewelry. In this picture, he mixed up all the music; his fingers wouldn't do what they were supposed to do. He would freeze from fright. He would be an utter failure.

I wonder if those people have any idea where we came from or what our lives were like before we boarded this ship?

I wonder if they care?

"Will you hurry up?" Ezra said. "Mr. Podoliak told us to be at the entrance to the ballroom at seven-thirty sharp."

"I'm almost ready." Jacob ran a comb through his hair. "I think my hair has grown at least four centimeters since we came on board."

"It must be all the blini you've been eating."

Jacob grinned. "Must be." He took one last glance at himself in the mirror. "All right. I'm as ready as I'll ever be."

"It's about time!"

♬

Mr. Greenblatt led the musicians along corridors and up and down stairs until they came at last to the first-class ballroom. Mr. Podoliak hurried the stragglers along at the end of the line.

As they approached the ballroom, Jacob heard the buzz of conversation, the clinking of cups and glasses, even snatches of jazz music the professional orchestra was playing.

He stood stock-still. He had never seen such an elegant room in his life—with its brocade wallpaper, shining chandeliers, and plush rugs. The chairs were upholstered in intricate patterns of damask. He smelled the women's flowery perfume and the men's tangy aftershave.

He gripped his mandolin case more tightly; afraid it might slip from his sweating hand. *This is it*, he thought. *I'll either sink or swim.* "Ezra, what do you think?"

"About what?"

"Do they throw bad musicians overboard?" He licked his lips. "To the sharks?"

"Your imagination is running away with you again."

Jacob swallowed hard. "I suppose so."

At the front of the room, the jazz musicians stopped playing and, with a gesture from their leader, picked up their instruments and began to leave the stage.

Ezra nudged Jacob. "Close your mouth."

"But they're—"

"Negro? I know," Ezra said. "So, close your mouth. You're acting like a country boy."

Jacob felt his face growing red. "I hope they didn't see me staring at them."

"They're probably used to it."

The mandolin players headed toward the chairs and music stands on the stage. Jacob noticed the captain speaking with Dr. Nowak, their heads close together, their faces serious.

Mr. Greenblatt stepped onto the platform, walked toward the microphone, and cleared his throat. "Ladies and gentlemen—"

A loud screeching sound erupted from the speakers. Everyone covered their ears. Mr. Greenblatt grimaced and stepped back. He cleared his throat and tried again. "Ladies and gentlemen, if I may have your attention please?"

The captain and Dr. Nowak stopped talking and turned to face Mr. Greenblatt. Gradually, the chatter died down.

"This evening for your listening pleasure, I present to you the young players of the mandolin orchestra from Mezritsh, Poland." He gestured to Mr. Podoliak. "Here is their teacher, Mr. Podoliak, to lead the orchestra." Mr. Greenblatt turned to face the musicians. "Do me proud, children," he whispered.

There was a scattering of polite applause as Mr. Podoliak made his way to the front and Mr. Greenblatt sat down on the chair reserved for him. He took his handkerchief out of his pocket and wiped his sweating face.

Estie the cat walked around the table and settled at Mr. Greenblatt's feet. He bent down and petted the cat absentmindedly.

While the players tuned their instruments, Jacob saw a stout man with a bushy mustache turn to his neighbor. "Looking forward to it, what?"

The thin man sitting beside him shrugged. "Those are the Jewish orphans. Right?"

Jacob thought the second man spoke with a different accent from the first one. *Is he from America?*

A middle-aged woman wearing a too-tight beaded dress leaned over to the thin man and said, "I hear they're heading to Canada."

The thin man gestured to a waiter. "Waiter! Another whiskey here!"

The woman sniffed. "As long as they're not coming to the United States." She held up her glass. "For me too, while you're at it."

"You Americans drink like fish," the stout man said.

Estie the cat walked over to the stout man, sat down on her haunches, and began to lick her fur.

The thin man downed his drink. "Drowning my worries." He glanced at the stout man. "You don't have hordes of unwashed immigrants flooding your shores."

"Except for the Indians, didn't everyone in America come from somewhere else?"

The thin man shrugged and leaned back on his chair. "It's a damn good thing President Coolidge put a stop to them a few years ago."

"They should all be sterilized," the woman said. "The whole lot of that inferior stock!"

Jacob couldn't hear the rest of what the woman was saying, but he wondered what "sterilized" meant. It did not sound like a good thing.

"Now, now," said the stout gentleman. "Isn't that taking things rather far?" He lit his cigar. "After all, moderation is good. Don't you agree?"

"Not in this case," the thin man said. "By the way, have you read—?"

Mr. Podoliak rapped on his music stand. "Ladies and gentlemen, silence please."

Chapter 19

Jacob's fingers tingled. He closed his eyes. He imagined the notes of the music in front of him, the chords, the vibrato, the familiar E, F#, G, G, G.

He breathed deeply, opened his eyes, and looked at Mr. Podoliak. His baton was raised. Jacob pressed his lips together. *Now we'll show those people how well Jewish orphans from Poland can play!*

He began to play. It felt almost as if the music were a part of his body. He played the first verse, and then the rest of the orchestra joined him in the chorus. They not only played the notes but everyone also sang the words that seemed to pull at his heart; to remind him of home.

Benjamin played the second verse, and Sula played the third one.

Az ir vet, kinder, elter vern, When you grow older, children,

Vet ir aleyn farshteyn, You will understand by yourselves,

Vifl in di oysyes lign trern, How many tears lie in these letters,

Un vi fil geveyn. And how much lament.

The piece was over. Silence. Then polite applause.

"The young ones are good, what?" the stout man said as he relit his cigar.

"Not bad," the thin man said. "But what was that language they were singing? Was it German?"

"I know German," his wife said. "That is definitely *not* German!"

"I believe it is called Yiddish. It comes from German," the stout man said. "Why, I once knew a Jewish tailor in London who—"

"Just what you'd expect from a mongrel race," the thin man said. "A mongrel language for a mongrel people."

"Excuse me," the stout man said as he stood up. "I think I will find another table." He furrowed his brow. "Where people are more congenial."

The thin man shrugged. "Do as you like."

"No skin off my back," his wife said.

Estie the cat growled deep in her throat and followed the stout man to another place in the room.

♪

"That didn't go so bad, did it?" Ezra said as the orphans gathered in their dining room after the performance. "And look at all the food the cook made for us!"

"I don't know." Jacob helped himself to a cream cheese sandwich. "I guess we played all right, but—"

"You were great!" Abe the Tall said as he slapped Jacob on the back, almost knocking the wind out of him.

"I was? Really?"

"Really!" Benjamin said.

"But did you hear what that couple was saying?" Abe the Tall said.

"I didn't understand everything, but I don't think it was good," Jacob said.

"What did they say?" David said.

"They were…calling us…." Abe the Tall pressed his lips together.

"What?" David said.

Abe the Tall shook his head.

"If it was something bad, I'll—" said Ezra.

"What?" Jacob said. "Go back to first class and beat them up?" The sandwich felt stuck in his throat.

"You're just a kid," Abe the Tall said.

"We all are," Jacob said.

"Didn't we have enough anti-Semites in Poland?" David said.

"Yeah. Do we have to have them on this ship, too?" Benjamin said.

Abe the Tall clenched his fists. "One day, maybe I'll leave Canada and go to *Eretz Yisroel*."

"You're right. Nobody will push us Jews around there," Benjamin said.

Memories of Bartek flashed through Jacob's mind. He crossed his arms and hugged his chest. "We have only one more day before we reach Canada. Let's not make any trouble."

"All right." Abe the Tall shrugged. "You're the star of the show. What you say, goes." He grinned. "I'll let you have the last word. At least, for now."

Chapter 20
Saturday June 25, 1927

"Jacob, wake up!"

"What is it?" Just in time, Jacob stopped himself from banging his head on the bottom of the upper bunk bed. He looked at Ezra through sleep-fogged eyes. "Is it Nathan? Is he better?" Jacob didn't want to ask the other question—the one that tied his stomach into knots.

"No. He's not."

"So—?"

"Don't worry about Nathan right now," Ezra said. "Mr. Greenblatt will take care of him. Meanwhile, listen." Ezra walked toward the door and opened it.

Jacob heard the sound of excited chatter, the clatter of people's shoes in the corridor, and a horn blowing in the distance.

"We're getting close to land." Ezra looked back at

Jacob. "I'm going up to the deck. Hurry and get dressed. I'll save a spot for you."

Land! What will this Canada be like? Jacob wondered. *What will I be like in this new country? Will I finally find a home?* His head buzzed with too many questions.

When Jacob was ready, he hurried along the corridor, clambered up the steps two at a time, and finally reached the upper deck where all the orphans and other third-class passengers stood pressed against the railings. The sun was rising in the east; Halifax spread out in the west from the harbor and beyond.

"Over here, Jacob!" Ezra said.

Gulls screeched overhead and water lapped against the ship's hull. The sun sparkled on the blue-gray water and lit up a green haze of land in the distance. Jacob gazed at the stout tugboats coming to pull the *Estonia* through the harbor and toward the pier. "Those boats remind me of a picture in Mrs. Adler's old book of nursery rhymes."

"Which one?" Ezra glanced at Jacob, not wanting to take his eyes off the scene in front of him. "You sure liked to stick your nose into her books!"

Jacob could still recall the musty smell of the old books in Mrs. Adler's library. He felt like crying but didn't know why.

"Did you hear me?" Ezra said. "Which one?"

Jacob shook his head, trying to rid himself of his cobweb memories. "Oh, the one of the old woman.... What's her name? The one with huge, billowing skirts and lots of children underneath. Do you remember?"

Ezra pointed as the city of Halifax came closer into view. "Isn't that a lot more interesting than some story in an old book?"

"You mean those wooden houses? Halifax looks almost like a *shtetl*, a village, back in Poland!"

The ship was a familiar place now. Jacob yearned to be on land, but at the same time, he began to worry about what lay ahead. Sea. Land. Here. There. Everything ran together in a terrifying blur.

Mr. Greenblatt joined the group. He was shaved and wore a clean shirt and freshly pressed suit. "Children," he said, "we are almost ready to dock. Go below now and get your things together." He swept his arm out beyond the ship. "You must always remember this day— when you began a new chapter in your lives!"

Mr. Podoliak wagged a finger at them. "But whatever you do," he said, "don't forget your mandolins!"

♪

"Are you coming?" Ezra said.

"I'll be right there," Jacob said. "I want to ask Mr. Greenblatt something."

"Okay," Ezra said, using his favorite new English word. "I'll see you in the cabin."

Jacob walked toward Mr. Greenblatt, who was leaning against the railing and looking at the city.

"Mr. Greenblatt?"

"Yes?" Mr. Greenblatt turned around.

Jacob swallowed hard. "Sir, please tell me about Nathan. How is he?"

Mr. Greenblatt put his hand on Jacob's shoulder. "Now, I don't want you to worry about Nathan." He fiddled with his tie. "I already made arrangements for him."

"But what *are* they?"

Mr. Greenblatt cleared his throat and looked off into the distance. "I contacted the Canadian immigration officials. They agreed to let Nathan go to the hospital here until…he is better."

"And then?" Jacob bit his lower lip. He didn't want to ask what might happen if Nathan didn't get better.

Mr. Greenblatt shrugged. "And then, God willing, the good people in the Jewish community here will take care of him."

"Really? You mean, he might be able to stay? And even…maybe…be adopted?"

Mr. Greenblatt smiled a tight smile. "We can only hope."

PART THREE
THE NEW WORLD

Oh, sing for him
God's little song-birds
since his mother
cannot find him.

—POLISH FOLK SONG

Chapter 21

The cool morning breeze coming in from the ocean held the promise of rain. Jacob stood at the top of the crowded gangway along with the other orphans. He shivered. This gangway would take them from the ship to the Halifax pier; it was like a bridge from the old world to the new.

"Stay together, children," Mr. Greenblatt said. "And be sure you are wearing your name tags!"

Mr. Hansen, the chief steward, stood at the top of the gangway. Estie the cat was at his feet, as if she were getting ready to say good-bye to the passengers. "No reason to push or shove," Mr. Hansen said. "Everyone will leave in good order, in groups of one hundred. The new pier is not ready yet, but you will be processed at Pier Two. A good facility." He gazed at the orphans. "I have not seen much of you during this voyage...." His mouth crinkled in a smile. "But I wish you well in this new land."

"Thank you for all your help," Mr. Greenblatt said.

Mr. Hansen tipped his cap and moved to another group of passengers eager to disembark.

"Children, I will meet you in the reception hall," Mr. Greenblatt said. "I must go now to speak to the Canadian medical officer." He gestured behind him. "See? He is walking up the gangway right now."

Mr. Podoliak frowned. "I hope he will take Nathan to the hospital first."

Jacob clenched his fists. "He'd better!" He stood on tiptoe, but Mr. Greenblatt had disappeared in the crowd.

"What is that doctor looking for?" Ezra asked.

Jacob shrugged. "I don't know."

"Maybe to check if we're bringing any diseases to Canada," Alex said.

"Maybe," Sula said.

After several long minutes, the doctor finished his inspection. The crowd began to surge down the gangway.

"Children, keep track of your belongings—your suitcase and your mandolin, if you are in the orchestra," Mr. Podoliak said. "And don't forget jackets and caps!"

Jacob's legs trembled as he set his feet onto land after

ten days at sea. The land seemed to move, as if he were still on the ship. He walked with the other orphans to a large reception hall where some men in uniforms were seated behind desks. *Will we really be allowed to enter this country?* He shuddered. *Or, will we be sent back?*

Jacob sat down on a wooden bench and waited.

♪

All around him, Jacob heard people talking in many different languages—English, Yiddish, Polish, Russian—and some languages he didn't recognize. Some people sat quietly and stared straight ahead as they clutched their documents. Others kept up a steady stream of chatter. He heard laughter, loud talk, crying babies, children's shouts. In the rafters above his head, he heard the cooing of pigeons and the beating of wings.

Is everyone as nervous as I am? Jacob wondered.

A woman in a long, gray dress approached the group. "I am a Sister of Service," she said. "I am here to help you." She handed each of the orphans a small paper bag.

"Thank you," Jacob said in his best English.

"I'm glad you've already learned some English!" The woman smiled and then continued along the row.

Jacob opened the bag and shook out the contents: a sewing kit, a bar of soap, and a toothbrush. More intriguing was a box that made a rattling sound when he shook it.

All around him, Jacob heard the sound of tearing cardboard.

Ezra was already opening his box. "What does it say?"

"Let me see." Jacob tried to make out the English words. "Kell...ogg's...." He shook his head. "I don't know what that means."

"What about the rest?" Benjamin said.

"Corn...that's *papshoy*...and Flakes...*shneylech*...I think," Jacob said.

"Corn? They're giving us *corn* to eat?" Perla said.

"Corn is what they give to chickens back home!" Rose said.

"Feh! We're not chickens!" Benjamin said.

"We're *people!*" Abe the Tall said.

With that, the orphans looked at each other and, one by one, unceremoniously dumped the boxes onto the floor.

"Weiss. Jacob Weiss," an immigration officer called.

As Jacob made his way to the desk at the front of the room, all he could hear was the beating of his heart and the crunch of cornflakes under his feet.

Chapter 22

Jacob handed his documents to the immigration official. The man examined them carefully. Jacob bit his lip. *Is everything all right?* he wondered. *Will the man let me come in?*

The man pointed to where Jacob had to sign his name on a form. With shaking fingers, Jacob signed his name and handed the form back to the man.

The man took the paper, looked up, and smiled. "Welcome to Canada."

Jacob nodded and, with trembling legs and a huge grin, made his way back to where the other orphans were standing.

Ezra slapped him on the back. "You made it!"

Jacob shrugged. "Of course, I did."

"Nein! Ich vill nit! Ich ken nit!" David's cries filled the reception hall. "I don't want to! I can't!"

Everyone stopped talking and stared at David. Mr. Greenblatt hurried over to where David was standing in front of the official. "What has happened? What is the problem?"

The official pointed at David. "Look here. This boy won't sign his name to the document." The man shook his head. "If he doesn't sign it, he won't be admitted to Canada."

Mr. Greenblatt frowned. "David, why will you not sign the paper?" he said in Yiddish.

David hung his head. "*S'iz Shabbos.* It is the Sabbath."

Jacob could see David's Adam's apple going up and down as the boy tried to swallow. "I cannot write on Shabbos. It is a sin."

Mr. Greenblatt took off his hat and wiped his brow with his handkerchief. "But…but you *have* to, or they won't let you into Canada!"

"Sir, what is going on?" the official said. "Why won't the boy sign the paper?"

Mr. Greenblatt held up his hand. "Please. Wait one moment."

The official gestured toward the people sitting on the benches. "All right, but a lot of people want their turn."

"David," Mr. Greenblatt said, "it is just a piece of paper." Jacob heard him mutter, "I was afraid something like this might happen."

David shook his head. "I cannot break the commandment to do no work on Shabbos." He sighed. "If that means I can't stay...."

"But...but...I made all the arrangements!" Mr. Greenblatt said. "How can you go back? And what will the Mezritsher Society say if I fail?"

David's eyes filled with tears. "If the streets are *trayfe*, not kosher, then maybe I shouldn't stay here after all."

Jacob had an idea. *It isn't brilliant*, he thought, *but maybe it will work.* He took a deep breath and walked over to David and Mr. Greenblatt. His heart was hammering in his chest.

"Mr. Greenblatt, I...I might have a solution."

"What? Tell me quick! The man is waiting."

"When does the train leave for Montreal?"

Mr. Greenblatt raised his eyebrows. "Our train leaves the station at eight-thirty sharp, but what does that have to do—"

"Maybe...maybe David can stay here in the reception hall—"

"But we have to catch the train!"

"David can wait here until Shabbos is over and then sign the paper and join the rest of us on the train."

"But…but he can't stay here by himself!"

"Of course he can! After all, he's nearly seventeen," Jacob said. "Right, David?"

David looked around the vast hall. "I…I guess so."

"Then, after Shabbos is over," Jacob said, "you can sign the paper."

"But…but where will you be?"

"We'll be waiting for you on the train."

"Maybe it will work." Mr. Greenblatt turned toward the official and explained Jacob's idea.

The man stroked his chin. "Well, I don't see why not. I'm a Christian myself. Wouldn't do anything against the Lord's Day."

Mr. Greenblatt put a hand on David's shoulder. "Sit back down and, when Shabbos is over, sign the paper and hurry to catch the train."

"You'd better be on that train!" Jacob said.

"I will," David said. "I promise."

♫

"Follow me, children," Mr. Podoliak said as he led the group along a corridor, down a set of stairs, and into the Canadian National Railway waiting room.

Small shops lined one wall—money exchange, newspapers, tobacco, candy. Along another wall was a cafeteria from which came the tantalizing smells of good food cooking.

Mr. Podoliak fumbled in his briefcase and pulled out a small pouch. He cleared his throat and raised his hand for quiet. "Mr. Greenblatt told me to give each of you two Canadian quarters, worth fifty cents, for spending money for the train trip."

"Gosh, that's swell," Ezra said, using more of his favorite new English words.

Jacob grasped the two hard coins in his hand. The warmth of the coins seemed to spread from his hand to the rest of his body. *My own spending money*, he thought. *This must be a wonderful country.*

"Who's that on the front of the coin?" Ezra said.

"He's the king of England," Jacob said.

"Canada has a king?" Ezra said.

Jacob nodded. "Sure does. King George the fifth."

Ezra furrowed his brow. "How do you know that?"

Jacob blushed. "I guess I read it somewhere."

"I don't care who's on the money," Abe the Tall said. "I'm starving!"

"So am I," Benjamin said.

"Let's go," Abe the Tall said.

With these words, the orphans rushed over to the cafeteria where they discovered the wonders of spaghetti (some of them), hot dogs (a few of them), and bananas (all of them) for the first time in their lives.

Chapter 23

A driving rain began to fall as the orphans hurried to board the train. The lights from the lampposts shone on the puddles beside the tracks. The air was filled with white steam and gray coal smoke pouring from the exhaust stacks on top of the huge locomotive.

"It's a flood!" Benjamin said.

"Like in Noah's time," Abe the Tall said.

"Our clothes are getting soaked!" Rose and Perla said.

"It's raining cats and dogs," Ezra said, trying out another English expression he'd learned.

The kids laughed, as they imagined cats and dogs pouring down on them.

Jacob's stomach was churning. *Where is David? Will he miss the train because of what I said? Or, will he break*

Shabbos to get on the train and blame that on me? I tried to help, but maybe I only made things worse.

He balled his hands into fists. *Like when I tried to help Nathan on the ship and only made things worse.*

"Come on!" Ezra said. "Why are you dragging your feet?"

"I...I'm going to wait for David." Jacob fumbled with the buttons of his jacket.

"Don't! You'll miss the train!"

"I feel responsible." Jacob finally managed to do up his jacket. He shivered. The cold damp was seeping through to his skin.

Ezra placed his hands on Jacob's shoulders. The rain dripped from the boys' caps onto their faces. "You mean, after coming all this way, you're going to get left behind right here, at the first place we land in Canada?"

Jacob brushed Ezra's hands away. "It was my idea. If David gets left behind, it'll be my fault."

"What's going on?" Mr. Greenblatt bustled toward the pair, followed by Mr. Podoliak. "I've got your tickets. Let's go!"

"But what about David?" Jacob said.

"I'm worried about him, too," Mr. Podoliak said.

"We can't delay our journey just because of one boy," Mr. Greenblatt said.

"See?" Ezra said.

"But—" Jacob said.

"No buts," Mr. Greenblatt said. "If he misses the train, then he'll have to take the next one." He gestured behind him. "Don't worry. I talked to the ticket agent and made the arrangements."

"All right," Jacob said. "If you're sure…."

"Of course, I'm sure," Mr. Greenblatt said.

A train whistle pierced the air. The conductor yelled, "All aboard!"

"We'd better board the train," Mr. Podoliak said, "or we'll *all* be left behind!"

Jacob and Ezra walked up the three steps onto the train and settled into their seats.

"I still don't like it," Jacob said.

There was a jerk as the brakes were released. The train whistle blew its warning blast. As the train began to move, Jacob felt the vibration of the iron wheels under the car and smelled the acrid smoke seeping in through the windows. Still no sign of David.

He could scarcely see outside as the rain sheeted against the pane. He pulled the window up and twisted his body to see better. The rain pelted on his face and ran down his neck onto his back. He pulled his jacket closer but it did little good.

Then he saw David running along the platform. His

mandolin case was in one hand and his suitcase in the other.

Jacob leaned out the window. "Hurry, David! Run!"

The other kids crowded around Ezra and Jacob.

"You can do it!" Abe the Tall yelled.

"You have to!" Benjamin called.

Suddenly, a gust of wind blew David's cap off his head. He stopped in his tracks, dropped his cases, and ran after his cap.

"What's he doing?" Ezra said. "He's going to miss the train because of a *cap*!"

"He's got to wear it!" Perla said.

"He's a religious boy," Rose said.

David scooped up the cap, plunked it on his head, grabbed his cases, and started after the train again.

"Hurry!" everyone shouted.

"Run like you've never run before!" Rose and Perla said together.

At the last minute, David threw his cases onto the platform of the car, clambered up the steps, and sank in a heap on the floor. He was gasping for breath; his cap and clothes were sopping wet.

The kids clapped and cheered.

Rose and Perla rushed to help him up.

"You made it!" Perla said.

"Just in time!" Rose said.

David could only nod as he staggered to his feet and collapsed into the nearest available seat.

"Now all we have to worry about," Sula said, "is whether Alex is going to throw up."

Chapter 24

As the train made its way across the darkening land, all Jacob could see was the occasional twinkle of yellow lights in a farmhouse or small village. Once, he spied a boy and his dog sitting by the side of the tracks and watching as the train sped by.

The children's chatter gradually died down as, one by one, they drifted off to sleep. Jacob took off his sodden jacket, rolled it into a ball, and placed it against the window to use as a pillow. The steady pulse of the train's wheels on the track lulled him to sleep.

He dreamed he was in a vast railway station. The ceiling was so high that he could not see the top; the walls were lined with thick marble. He heard the hands of a giant clock on a tall pillar in the middle of the hall. *Tick. Tock. Tick. Tock.* The black hands on the clock began to grow longer and longer. They reached out for him. They were trying to snatch him into the clock! He stepped away until he felt the cool marble wall on his back. All around him, people were pushing and shoving, hurrying every which way to catch their trains.

Jacob looked up at the board announcing the trains and their destinations, but the track numbers were garbled, jumbled up, confusing. He felt sick to his stomach.

He asked a man—who vaguely looked like the Mezritsher rabbi—where to catch the train to Canada. The old man stroked his beard. "Did I not tell you to go to Palestine or America? Is that not what I always said?" He raised a bony finger and pointed down a long corridor. "There," he said. "Go there."

As Jacob stumbled along the corridor, the walls began to close in on him. Where was everyone? Where were the other orphans? Jacob's head throbbed. He was alone. Abandoned. Small. He couldn't think. He couldn't move. He couldn't breathe.

The sharp blast of a train whistle startled Jacob awake. The train was arriving at a station. He looked out the window. A light shone on the word "CAMPBELLTOWN" on top of the building. He was shaking and the sweat poured into his eyes. He wiped his forehead with his sleeve. He shivered as he remembered the shreds of his nightmare.

"Where are we?" Ezra yawned and rubbed his eyes. "I feel like a pretzel after sleeping on that hard seat all night."

Jacob took a shaky breath. "It's better than—"

"What's wrong? Why are you croaking like a frog?"

Jacob cleared his throat. "Nothing. I had a bad dream." He paused. "Anyway, this is better than the train from Mezritsh," he said. "Or from Warsaw."

Ezra patted the green plush seat. "More padding."

"I'm thirsty," Benjamin said.

"I'm hungry," Abe the Tall said.

"You're always hungry," Benjamin said.

Mr. Podoliak stood up in front of the group. His suit was crumpled and his tie was askew. "Children, during the night, we traveled through the provinces of Nova Scotia and New Brunswick." He swept his arm out. "We are now crossing the border into the province of Québec. They speak French here."

"French?" Perla said.

"I don't even know English yet!" Rose said.

Mr. Podoliak shook his head. "Not to worry," he said. "We are heading for Ontario. People speak English there."

"That's a relief," the girls said.

Mr. Podoliak gestured toward the end of the car. "Please wash your hands and use the facilities. Afterwards,

I'll hand out the sandwiches the Halifax Jewish women gave us."

"I think I'll pass," Alex said, who was looking rather green in the face.

Sula nodded. "Good idea."

"Have you seen the bathroom yet?" Rose said.

"Disgusting!" Perla said.

"I don't know what's worse—the outhouse back home or the thing here they call a toilet."

"Nothing but a hole over the tracks," Perla whispered. "And the sink is like a tiny bowl."

Rose stood up. "Come on, Perla. We don't have a choice."

"That's for sure."

Soon afterwards, as the kids were munching on their sandwiches, Mr. Greenblatt opened the door to their car. *How does he always manage to look so neat and clean?* Jacob wondered. *Even his shoes are shining!*

"It must be nice," Ezra whispered, "to be in a first-class compartment."

"And a sleeper car, too," Jacob said.

"Children," Mr. Greenblatt said, "I just want to tell you that there will be a welcoming committee in Montreal."

"Another one?" Abe the Tall said.

"Don't you like being a celebrity?" Benjamin said as he elbowed his friend.

Abe the Tall grunted. "I can do without all that stuff."

"Me too," David said.

Mr. Greenblatt held up his hand. "Please be on your best behavior. The success of the Jewish Farm School depends on you."

"What does he mean?" Ezra said.

"I don't know," Jacob said, "but I have a feeling we'll soon find out."

Chapter 25

"Are we there yet?" Ezra said. The group had devoured the cheese and egg salad sandwiches, apples, and cookies. They started to throw the wrappings at each other when Mr. Podoliak rapped with his baton on top of one of the seats. "Time for practice. I don't want you to get rusty."

"I want to play checkers," Abe the Tall said.

"Later, my boy," Mr. Podoliak said. "Now, players, take out your mandolins." He gazed up and down the aisle. "I know this isn't an ideal situation, but we have to do the best we can."

For the next hour, the children practiced the pieces they had played in the concert on the *Estonia*.

"Watch your tremolo, girls," Mr. Podoliak said to Rose and Perla.

"Sula, is your mandolin in tune?"

"Benjamin, sit up straight."

"Jacob, you are improving."

"Alex, take it easy on the cymbals. We don't want you to overpower the mandolins."

"Abe, why did I ever allow you to play the drums?"

After an hour, Jacob's fingers felt numb and the notes began to blur in front of his eyes.

"All right," Mr. Podoliak said. "That's enough for today."

The kids cheered.

Mr. Podoliak held up his hands. "I was planning to give you some new pieces when we arrived at the farm school, but I want to give one of them to you now." He reached into his briefcase and pulled out sheets of music. "Please study this piece every chance you get. It is called 'El Capitan' by the American composer, John Philip Sousa." He frowned. "When we get to the farm school, we must do a lot of rehearsing, in spite of the farm work and your regular schooling."

Ezra raised his hand. "Sir, do you mean we have to go to school along with the farm work?"

"Of course, you do!" Mr. Podoliak said. "Did you think you were going to a terrible workhouse, like in a Dickens novel?"

"Well…I didn't know," Ezra said.

"We are Jews." Mr. Podoliak seemed to stand taller. "Remember, we are the People of the Book." He paused. "That means *many* books, not only the Torah."

♫

For the rest of the day, the kids read, played cards, practiced their music, or dozed. Jacob played (and lost) a game of checkers with Abe the Tall. From time to time, Mr. Greenblatt looked in on the kids, but most of the time, he stayed with the other first-class passengers.

The train sped along a sparkling blue bay dotted with tiny fishing villages, and then through a valley filled with ripening fields of barley and hay, vegetable gardens, and apple orchards. Jacob could almost imagine he was in Poland again. He shook his head. *It is here I want to be*, he thought, *not in that old land filled with sadness.*

He remembered how Mrs. Adler had once arranged for the children to go to the local movie house. They had watched a movie with Charlie Chaplin called *The Kid*. It was about a man, a tramp, who found an abandoned baby and adopted him. Rose and Perla cried when the orphan child was taken from the tramp. (Jacob had had a lump in his throat.) The boys cheered when the tramp climbed up on the rooftops and tried to catch up with the truck that was taking the child away. Everyone clapped when man and child were reunited at the end.

Jacob never forgot the slightly sick but excited feeling as he watched the images in the movie pass in front of his eyes—faster than anything he'd seen before. Now, the landscape speeding past him was like that movie from long ago.

When at last the train traveled over the Victoria Bridge, Jacob's heart beat faster. The lights of the city of Montreal made the evening sky glow as the train slowed down and finally came to a stop.

"Bonaventure Station," Mr. Podoliak said. "It means 'good adventure' in French." He smiled. "I hope this will be a good adventure for us all."

Chapter 26

"Take all your suitcases and instruments," Mr. Podoliak said. "We need to find the welcoming committee and then change trains for the last part of our journey."

"I wish we didn't have to be 'welcomed' so much," Ezra said.

"Me too," Jacob said. "I just want to get there already!"

"Now, boys," Mr. Greenblatt said. "It's not that bad. These are Canadian Jews who want to help the farm school."

"Yes, but—"

"No buts. We need all the support we can get." He spread his hands out, palms up. "Do you think money grows on trees?"

"No, but—"

"Please, boys, do as I ask," Mr. Greenblatt said. "Then everything will be all right. Okay?"

"Okay." Jacob liked the sound of this new English word.

The orphans gathered together on a platform near an empty track. A photographer took their photo with the welcoming committee, people made speeches, and then they were hurried onto another platform and boarded their train for Toronto.

The train whistle blew; the train began to move out of the station.

"I'm getting tired of all this traveling!" Ezra said.

"It feels like we've been on this trip forever," Jacob said.

"It's been *days* since we had a bath or changed our clothes," Perla said.

Rose held her nose. "I think we're starting to smell."

"Patience, children," Mr. Podoliak said. "We should arrive in Toronto in the morning, and then it will be only a short train ride to Georgetown." He smiled. "Meanwhile, I've got a real treat for you."

"What?"

Mr. Podoliak opened two large paper bags from which wafted a delicious aroma. "Fresh from Dunn's Famous Restaurant in Montreal. Paid for by those people you didn't want to meet." He began to hand out their supper: smoked meat sandwiches (still warm) on rye bread, coleslaw, potato chips, dill pickles, and bottles of a fizzy drink.

A few minutes later, Ezra burped and held out his empty bottle. "I like this drink." He read the label aloud. "Orange Crush. If this is what we get in Canada, I'm all for it!"

Benjamin rubbed his stomach. "Now *that's* what I call a good meal."

"And it was even kosher," David said.

"So much food," Abe the Tall said. "It must be true that in this country the streets are paved with gold."

"I haven't seen any gold yet," Jacob said, "but this is a good start."

♫

The next morning, the group finally arrived at Union Station in Toronto. The conductor walked through their car and said, "Last stop, ladies and gentlemen, boys and girls. Welcome to Toronto! Make sure you take all your belongings with you."

"Sir," Mr. Podoliak said, "can you tell me where we take the train to Georgetown?"

The conductor scratched his head. "Georgetown? That will be the Brampton line." He pointed out the window. "You're lucky. You won't have to walk to the new station because it's not ready for passengers yet. You can board your train right here."

The kids piled into a railway car and before they knew it, they had arrived at the Georgetown station.

Several trucks were waiting for them. After a short ride, they arrived at the gate of the farm. Over the gate hung a banner in Yiddish and English saying,

CANADIAN JEWISH FARM SCHOOL
WELCOME MEZRITSH ORPHANS

The kids got out of the trucks and stood at the gate. "What do we do now?" Ezra said.

"Look," Jacob said. "It looks like another welcoming committee."

A tall, husky man stood at the gate, along with some other people. He wore a dark suit and a floppy hat. He kept pulling on his tie, as if he'd rather be wearing something else.

Mr. Greenblatt led the group to the man. "Children," he said, "meet Mr. Morris Saxe."

Chapter 27
September 1927

"I've never been so tired in my life!" Ezra plopped down onto his bed in the boys' dormitory.

Jacob was sitting on the edge of his bed practicing scales on his mandolin. He looked over at his friend. "Did you imagine, when we came here three months ago, that we would be so busy?"

Ezra shook his head. "Not in a million years!"

Jacob placed his mandolin on his bed, stood up, and walked toward the window. All around the farm, the leaves on the trees were changing color to burnished reds and golds and falling onto the ground. The days were warm, but the nights were cool. Mr. Saxe called this season "Indian Summer"—the warm spell before "real winter" set in.

Jacob shivered when he thought of the coming ice

and snow. Mr. Greenblatt had warned them that the winter here would be much colder than in Mezritsh. "I'm glad Mrs. Saxe ordered more blankets for us."

Ezra propped his head on his hand. "She's a nice woman. Always thinking about us. She works so hard. And what a great cook!"

Jacob grinned. "It's a good thing Mrs. Adler didn't have to cook. I think she would have burned everything!"

"That's for sure." Ezra sighed. "Still, between farm work in the morning, school in the afternoon, more farm work in the evening, and mandolin practice the rest of the time, we barely have time for ourselves."

"What would you do with the extra time?"

Ezra lay back down, bent his arms, and put his head on his palms. "I don't know. Maybe go to the moving pictures in town or listen to the radio more." He started to hum a tune under his breath. "You know how Mr. Saxe invites a few of us to go to his house on Saturday night?"

"He treats us like family. And his daughter, Leona? She's only three years old." He swallowed hard. "She reminds me of my sister, Raisele."

"Last time I went, he let me listen with the head-phones to the radio. There was a show from Chicago that was on." Ezra smiled. "I had to take turns with their son, Percy. He wanted to listen, too."

"Last time I was there, all I heard was a lot of buzzing and static."

"It must have been a clear night when I was there. Anyway, they played some songs I like." He sat up and began to sing the words of a new popular song.

Jacob turned away from the window and leaned against the wall. "Do you ever want to go back to Mezritsh?"

"Not on your life!" Ezra sat up. "And waste all the English I've learned so far?" He paused and began to speak in English. "Listen to this one. 'By golly.' Good expression. Right?"

Jacob walked back to his bed and sat down. "Right." He began to speak in Yiddish again. "Seriously, English is so hard—"

"—Sometimes I think my head will explode," Ezra agreed.

"But you're the best of all of us!" Jacob said.

Ezra shrugged. "I'm trying."

"You're lucky, you know," Jacob said. "You get to take care of the horses."

Ezra smiled. "I like them. It's almost like they know what to do before I even tell them."

"It's better than taking care of all those smelly chickens like the girls do."

"Or washing a ton of dishes!"

Jacob looked at his hands. "You know, at first I was worried I wouldn't be able to play the mandolin because of all the milking I do. Twice a day, every day." He flexed his fingers. "But it looks like I can milk cows and still play." He smiled when he remembered the warmth of the cows, the sloshing of the milk into the pails; how accepting the cows had been at first of his fumbling fingers.

The farm cat always seemed to know when it was milking time. Jacob had learned how to squirt the milk from the cow's teat directly into the cat's mouth. He loved to hear her purring like a little engine while she licked her fur afterwards.

"You're one of our best players. You know that, don't you?"

Jacob felt his face growing red. He hoped what Ezra said was true. "Thanks," he mumbled.

A loud bell rang from the kitchen below.

"Come on," Jacob said. "Time for supper."

Ezra rubbed his belly. "Mrs. Saxe can probably hear my stomach rumbling all the way down the stairs and into the kitchen."

♫

Everyone was seated on benches on either side of long tables. The two hired kitchen helpers, along with a few of the girls who were on waitress duty, were serving the meal.

"Eat up, everyone," Rose said as the helpers walked with laden trays between the tables.

"We made a huge pot of soup from the vegetables in the garden," Perla said.

"Tomatoes, carrots, onions, potatoes—"

"A million vegetables!"

Alex slurped his soup noisily and wiped his mouth with the back of his sleeve.

"Alex!" Sula said. "Eat like a human being!"

"Sorry," Alex said. "But it's so good!"

"I know. But you're in Canada now, not on a deserted island." Sula sighed. "You have to have some manners!"

Alex only nodded, for he was busy chewing on a piece of bread.

Ezra emptied his glass of milk and reached for the jug. "I'm glad Mr. Saxe has lots of cows. We can drink all the milk we want."

"Only twenty!" Jacob said. "Pass the jug when you're done."

Everyone was talking, laughing, eating, and drinking. *Are we the sad, scrawny orphans who arrived only three months ago?* Jacob thought.

Mr. Podoliak stood up and rapped on his glass with a knife. Everyone stopped talking and turned to face him. "Children," he said, "I have an important announcement."

He glanced at Mr. Saxe, who was standing by the door. Mr. Saxe wore blue overalls held up by suspenders. His shirt sleeves were rolled up above his elbows and a battered hat sat on his head. He nodded at Mr. Podoliak.

Mr. Podoliak cleared his throat. "Because you have been practicing so hard and have improved so much, Mr. Greenblatt and I have decided that the mandolin orchestra is ready to give a public concert."

Rose screeched.

Perla clapped.

"Where?" Benjamin said.

"When?" Abe the Tall asked.

"I'm not ready," David protested.

"Look at Alex," Ezra whispered. "He's starting to look green."

"He ate too fast," Sula said.

"He's probably dreading the train ride," Jacob said.

Mr. Podoliak held up his hands. "Quiet, please," he said. "We have arranged a small concert in Toronto to raise money for our farm school—one in Toronto in October, and the other in Detroit in November.

"And then in April...." He straightened his back. "The most important one of all...at Carnegie Hall in New York City." He paused and gazed at the children. "I'm very proud of you," he said. "You've come very far in the last few months."

"I read about Carnegie Hall," Jacob piped up. "Mr. Andrew Carnegie gave heaps of money to build it." He paused. "I think, about thirty years ago."

Benjamin scratched his head. "This Mr. Carnegie must be very rich."

"Rich like King Solomon who built the Temple in Jerusalem," David said.

Jacob shrugged. "Maybe richer."

"And we get to play in his Hall!" Ezra said.

"Carnegie Hall is historic," Mr. Podoliak said. "Great symphony orchestras like the New York Philharmonic have played there, plus fine musicians like the violinist Fritz Kreisler and the pianist Sergei Rachmaninoff."

He took his handkerchief out of his pocket and wiped his brow. "Nothing to worry about," he said, "but we will need extra rehearsals to get ready."

"Right," Ezra whispered. "Between taking care of the horses and—"

"—Milking the cows!" Jacob said.

Mr. Podoliak furrowed his brow. "And if we are lucky, we will raise enough money to maintain this wonderful school." He glanced at Mr. Saxe again. "For one more year, and maybe even two."

"Let's hope." Mr. Saxe shook his head as he turned and hurried out the door.

Jacob stared at the closed door. *Isn't there enough money to keep the farm school going? If there isn't, what will happen to us?*

Chapter 28

The next six months passed in a whirl for Jacob. He felt as if he was leading two separate lives. He moved between two separate calendars—one Jewish, one "secular," as the rabbi called it.

In the fall, a rabbi came from Toronto to conduct the services for the Jewish High Holidays. *Sukkot*, the autumn Jewish harvest festival followed soon afterwards. Mr. Saxe and a few of the older boys built a *sukkah* behind the dormitory. It was the flimsy shelter where the children took turns to eat their meals.

The rabbi explained, "The sukkah is supposed to remind us of the time God took care of the Israelites in the wilderness after they were freed from slavery in Egypt."

"Like when we got out of Poland?" Ezra said.

The rabbi frowned. "Not exactly."

That year of 1927, Sukkot came at the same time as Thanksgiving. Mrs. Saxe, the two cooks, and some of the girls helped prepare the feast: roast turkey, stuffing, mashed potatoes with gravy, sweet potatoes, cranberry sauce, sweet corn, squash, apple cake, and pumpkin pie.

"I don't think I've ever eaten so much in my life," Jacob said as he pushed his empty plate away.

Ezra burped loudly. "Me neither!"

Jacob glanced over at the girls' plates. "Why didn't you eat any turkey?"

"I can't," Perla said.

"It's good!" David said. "It's even kosher!"

"I can't either," Rose said. "After taking care of the chickens and turkeys, I can't imagine eating one!"

Benjamin helped himself to another slice of turkey. "You don't know what you're missing!"

♫

"The cows don't care if I get soaking wet," Jacob said as he hung up his damp jacket and warmed his hands by the stove. "Morning and night, morning and night, like clockwork they need to be milked."

"I know what you mean." Ezra looked up from his schoolwork. "I have to feed and water the horses every day."

Jacob shivered. "But I guess if some of us boys didn't do the milking, then we wouldn't have all that good milk, butter, and cheese."

"And Mr. Saxe wouldn't have anything to sell at his creamery." Ezra glanced at Jacob. "What's the matter?"

"I…I don't know. I can't stop shaking."

Ezra stood up and grabbed Jacob's sleeve. "Maybe you should go up to bed." He pushed Jacob toward the stairs. "I'll get Mrs. Saxe."

"But—"

"No buts, my friend."

Jacob did not have the strength to argue. He plodded up the stairs, staggered to his bed, and plopped down in a heap. *I'll close my eyes for just a minute.*

He dreamed he saw his sister, Raisele, sitting beside him. She was playing with her rag doll, but when she looked up, her eyes were empty sockets.

"Raisele?"

"Jacob, come with me to Mama and Papa," Raisele said. "It's nice there. Quiet. Peaceful." She started to hum a strange tune—an echo of a song Jacob knew but couldn't exactly place.

A sob rose in Jacob's throat. *It would be so good to see Mama and Papa again!*

"Come with me," Raisele said. "Come with me." She reached out her arms, but as she did, the skin fell away

from her face, her arms, her body. All that remained was a bony skeleton. "Jacob, are you coming? We have to hurry…."

Jacob shook his head and thrashed about. "Leave me alone!" he cried. "I want to live!"

Raisele began to fade away. Jacob thought he heard her say, "*Zay gezunt.* Be well. Good-bye," before she disappeared.

Jacob felt someone shake him gently on the shoulder.

"Jacob, wake up!" Mrs. Saxe said.

Ezra was standing beside Mrs. Saxe. "You must have had a bad dream."

"I guess so."

Mrs. Saxe furrowed her brow. "Too much sickness now, with all these colds and flu going around. The fall is hard and soon it will be winter," she muttered. "And these poor children have already suffered so much for so many years."

She put her hand on Jacob's forehead. "You have a fever," she said. "I'll make a mustard plaster to draw out the fever." She wagged her finger at Jacob. "And you, young man, get into your pajamas."

She leaned over and whispered in Ezra's ear. "Help your friend. I don't think he can manage by himself." She paused. "And I'll bring another blanket."

With these words, Mrs. Saxe bustled out of the room.

The next few days passed in a blur for Jacob. He vaguely remembered the heat of a wet mustard plaster on his chest and back; trying to swallow some chicken soup; even having to pee in the chamber pot because he was too weak to make it to the toilet.

One morning, Jacob opened his eyes. His head felt clearer. He could hear birds twittering outside and the sound of children's voices below.

"It's about time you got up!" Ezra said.

"How long have I been sick?" Jacob sat up in bed, rubbed his eyes, and rolled over to the side of the bed. "I want to get dressed."

"Come on," Ezra said. "Give me your hand. I'll help you."

"I don't need help."

"You sure do!" Ezra held his arm out. "You've been sick for days and days!"

Jacob noticed the dark circles under Ezra's eyes. "And you've been here all this time?"

Ezra shrugged. "Sure! That's what friends are for."

"I wish I could have helped Nathan more than I did." Jacob paused. "Do you think he's all right in Halifax?"

"He must be," Ezra said. "Probably so busy with his new family, he doesn't even think about us anymore."

"Maybe," Jacob said. "But I still think about him."

"Stop worrying so much," Ezra said. "All you need to think about now is getting better."

After Jacob got washed and dressed, he slowly made his way down the stairs, holding onto the railing with one hand and Ezra's arm with the other.

"Look!" Abe the Tall stood up and hurried toward Jacob. "It's like you've woken up from a long sleep."

"Are you hungry?" Sula said.

"I could eat a horse," Jacob said.

"Not kosher!" David said.

"Leave it to the 'rabbi' to have the last word," Abe the Tall said.

"I'm glad you're better," Perla said.

"Just in time for Hallowe'en," Rose said.

♪

"I can't believe we got free candy," Ezra said as the children walked along the streets of Georgetown.

Mr. Saxe smiled. "You see? All you had to do was shout 'Trick or Treat!' and the people opened their doors and put candy or apples into your bags."

"What does that mean, 'Trick or Treat?'" David shook his head. "This English is too hard."

"It means they must give you a treat or you will trick them," Mr. Saxe said.

"What kind of trick?" Ezra said.

Mr. Saxe scratched his head. "Well, like—"

Abe the Tall spit out a toffee candy. "They're disgusting." He began to pick his teeth. "No wonder they're free!"

"Almost as bad as those cornflakes they gave us in Halifax," Benjamin said.

"I won't eat them," David said. "Not kosher."

"Don't worry," Abe the Tall said. "You're not missing a thing."

Ezra took a bite of a candy apple. "These are delicious." He handed his half-eaten apple to Jacob. "Try it."

Jacob shook his head. "No thanks. I've got my own." He gazed at the carved faces of jack-o-lanterns lit up by glowing candles. *Hallowe'en isn't a Jewish holiday*, he thought, *but it's definitely a lot of fun.*

Chapter 29

On the following day, when everyone was feeling a little sick from eating candy, their English teacher, Mr. Curtin, rapped on his desk. "Students, I have an important announcement."

Everyone looked up from their reading or writing work.

"In one week, on Monday November seventh, it will be Armistice Day," Mr. Curtin said.

"What is that?" David said.

"Shh," Sula said. "Listen."

Mr. Curtin cleared his throat. "Armistice Day is the day we remember when the Great War ended." He paused. "The war to end all wars."

"I was just a little kid then," Benjamin whispered.

"Me too," Abe the Tall said.

"I realize that you are still learning English, but I have a special task for you," Mr. Curtin said. "John McCrae, a Canadian soldier, wrote a moving poem about the war. It's called 'In Flanders Fields.' On November seventh, you will join the students at the Georgetown high school to recite this poem."

Alex raised his hand.

"Yes?"

"But sir, this English is too hard."

Mr. Curtin peered at the children over his round glasses. "I know that English is still challenging for you, but you have made good progress these last few months." He took his glasses off, wiped them with a clean handkerchief, and put them back on his nose.

"I'll tell you what," he said. "I'll explain the hard words in the poem. After that, you'll practice the poem every chance you get.

"Don't worry. I'll help you through this." Mr. Curtin smiled. "You're Canadian now, and this is part of our country's heritage." He picked up a pile of papers. "Perla. Rose. Please hand these copies out."

There was a buzz of conversation when Mr. Curtin gestured for silence. "Oh, by the way, Mr. Podoliak tells me that he also wants the mandolin players to play 'God Save the King' at the high school."

"Great!" Abe the Tall said.

"More work!" Benjamin added.

For the next few days, every time Jacob did the milking, he brought the poem with him to the barn. He lay it on top of an overturned pail and glanced at it from time to time. With each pull on the cow's teats, he recited some words:

> In Flanders fields...the poppies blow...
> Between the crosses...row on row...
> That mark our place...and in the sky...
> The larks...still bravely...singing...fly...

"Thank you, cows," he said at the end of the week. "You helped me a lot."

The cows only mooed as he carried the brimming milk pails away.

On November 7, Mr. Saxe arranged for two trucks to take the orphans to the Georgetown high school.

"I'm so nervous," Perla said.

"Me too," Rose said.

Jacob could feel his stomach tied in knots, but when everyone in the school auditorium stood up and recited the poem, a strange feeling came over him. *This feels right. This feels good.*

At the end of the ceremony, the mandolin players walked up to the stage. Benjamin plucked a string and the players checked their tuning.

"Teachers and students," Mr. Curtin said. "Please rise. The mandolin orchestra from the farm school will play 'God Save the King.'"

There was a loud clatter of shuffling shoes and scraping chairs. Then, as Mr. Podoliak raised his baton, the orchestra played, and everyone sang the anthem. When they sang the last verse, Jacob felt his eyes fill with tears.

> Lord make the nations see
> That men should brothers be
> And form one family
> The wide world o'er.

"I'm starting to feel like a Canadian," Jacob said as the trucks took them back to the farm.

"Me too," Ezra said.

"Especially when we played 'God Save the King.'"

"Do you think Canada will ever have a queen?" Sula said.

"Why not?" Jacob said. "We've had one before."

"Who?" Benjamin said.

"Queen Victoria, you numbskull!" Abe the Tall said. "Don't you ever listen during history class?"

Benjamin yawned. "I must have been sleeping just then."

"As usual," Abe the Tall said.

♪

That year in late December, everyone on the farm celebrated Hanukkah. Mr. Saxe set up the *hanukkiah*, a nine-branched candlestick, in the dining hall. Every night, David led the kids in reciting the blessing over the candles and then they sang and played songs like "Maoz Tsur"/"Rock of Ages" on their mandolins. Mrs. Saxe and her helpers kept busy grating potatoes and frying *latkes*, potato pancakes, to eat when they were finished.

On the eighth and last night of the holiday, as the orphans were eating latkes and drinking apple cider or milk, Mr. Saxe told them about the time he had served in the Russian cavalry in the war between Russia and Japan, over twenty years before. He even lifted up his pants' leg and showed them the scar on his leg and pushed back his hair to show the scar on his forehead.

"Ooh!" Rose said.

"Does it still hurt?" Perla asked.

Mr. Saxe shook his head. "Not anymore." He gazed into the distance. "But it took me a long time to recover. And I had the help of some good people." He then described how he had eventually left Ukraine and made his way—first to England and then to Canada; how he had worked as an interpreter for the Canadian government during the Great War.

He ended his story by saying, "I felt like a Maccabee when I was your age." He lifted his arms, as if embracing them all in a warm circle. "Children, be of good courage. Never give up."

Everyone stood up and cheered and sang, "For He's a Jolly Good Fellow!" Mr. Saxe blushed, patted the boys on the back or on the head, and told a few jokes.

After everyone had eaten their fill of latkes, Mr. Saxe said, "I've arranged a special treat for you."

"What?" Perla said.

"When?" Rose said.

"This evening, we'll go on a sleigh ride." Mr. Saxe smiled. "I want to show you the Christmas lights on the way to town," he said. "Some of our neighbors and people in town already have electricity."

"I'm going to stay near the warm stove," Sula said.

"Me too," a chorus of other voices piped up.

In the end, only eight boys went for the ride.

"Good," Ezra said. "Only one pair of horses to hitch up."

They had not gone far along the road when Jacob noticed a strange red tinge in the night sky. "Look, Mr. Saxe!"

"I wonder what that is," Mr. Saxe said. "It's not far off." He waved the switch over the horses' flanks. "Get up!" The horses picked up speed and the sleigh glided faster on its runners. Mr. Saxe called over his shoulder, "We'd better hurry. There might be trouble."

As the sleigh drew closer to their neighbor's farm, Jacob could see sparks flying in the air above him. The air smelled of smoke and ash. His eyes began to water.

The sleigh rounded a corner. Jacob could hear the crackle of flames, the pop of things exploding, wood crashing down somewhere. The farmhouse was ablaze.

Men were running from the house with furniture. Others were up on a ladder pouring water from buckets passed hand over hand by a line of people. Still others were leading bawling cows and neighing horses from the barn.

A crowd of older women and young children gathered a short distance from the barn. They beat at sparks with wet cloths to keep the fire from spreading.

"Come on, boys!" Mr. Saxe shouted. "We've got to help!" He tied the horses' reins to a nearby tree, jumped off the wagon, and joined the men.

The boys ran after him. Abe and Ezra joined the bucket line, David and Jacob ran to help pump water. They filled anything that might hold water, including milk cans and chamber pots. Benjamin hurried to the house and heaved a baby carriage and then a rocking chair away from the fire.

The night seemed endless; the buckets grew heavier.

Everyone kept coughing while black soot and ashes flew every which way in the air. Jacob's eyes burned, his mouth was dry, his throat was sore. And still the buckets passed from hand to hand.

At last, someone shouted, "It's done! It's over! The fire is out!"

A loud cheer filled the air. Everyone put down the buckets and collapsed onto the ground.

"Come on, boys," Mr. Saxe said. "If you sit down now, you'll never get up." He wiped his face with his sooty gloves. "Time to get home."

Ezra yawned. "I think I'll fall asleep as soon as my head touches the pillow."

But all Jacob could think of was the word *home*.

A few days later, their neighbors and some townspeople brought gifts of knitted toques, scarves, socks, and mittens; jams, cakes, and pies. "Just being neighborly toward the poor orphans," they said. "And to thank you all for your help during the fire."

Mr. Curtin took off his hat. "You know, some of the folks around here weren't so happy about you Jewish orphans coming here." He smiled and put his hat back on. "But now, I think they've changed their tune."

Chapter 30
April 1928

The orphans stood in scattered groups under the eaves of the dormitory building as they tried to stay out of the pelting rain. They were waiting for the truck to take them to Georgetown, where they would board the train to Toronto and then on to New York City.

Jacob's heart was beating like a hammer. He leaned against the building, paced back and forth, peered along the road, and then went back to his pacing.

"What's wrong?" Ezra said. "You're as jumpy as a grasshopper!"

Jacob shrugged. "I don't know." He kicked a pebble with his shoe. "In a way, I want to go to New York City. In another way, I don't want to go."

"So, what's the problem?" Ezra swept his arm toward

the farm, the house, the fields. "Don't you want to have a break from the farm for a while?"

"You mean, leave all these cows and chickens?" He pinched his nose. "And the lovely smells?"

"Then what are you worried about?"

Jacob stared off into the distance. "You know, I love playing the mandolin. It's just that…." He looked at the pile of bags and instrument cases in the driveway. "Wait a minute!"

He hurried to the pile and rummaged through them. His heart skipped a beat. "Where's my mandolin?" he shouted. "Has anyone seen it?"

"Look in the dining room," Abe the Tall said.

"Or in the barn," Benjamin said, "with your lovely cows."

"That's not funny," Jacob said.

"Maybe you left it in the dormitory," Ezra said, "when you were practicing."

"Right," Jacob said. "Must have." He turned to go inside, but then called over his shoulder, "Don't leave without me!" He rushed into the building and took the stairs two at a time to the boys' dormitory.

All week long, he had been preoccupied with what to pack: clean socks, shined shoes, his sheet music, but most of all, his mandolin. *How could I forget my mandolin? What was I thinking?*

He pushed the door open and ran past the row of beds. His mouth was dry, and his belly ached. Then he saw his mandolin. It was sitting on his bed, as if waiting for him like a loyal friend; as if to say, "Were you going to leave me behind?"

The sweat was pouring down his face, but Jacob brushed it away with the back of his sleeve. He grabbed the mandolin and began to retrace his steps. On the way back down the stairs, he heard Mr. Saxe and Mr. Greenblatt arguing in the dining room. Jacob stopped in his tracks. He knew he shouldn't eavesdrop, but somehow, he couldn't help himself.

"I told you when we started out," Mr. Saxe said. "I made an agreement with Mr. Charles Blair, the head of the immigration department in Ottawa." Someone pounded his fist on the table. Jacob inhaled sharply. "We have to follow all the rules. If not, the farm school will be finished, shut down, *kaput*."

There was a pause before Mr. Greenblatt answered. "Morris, don't worry so much. I'll take care of everything."

Jacob crept further down the stairs.

"What do you mean, you'll take care of everything?" Mr. Saxe was shouting now. Jacob couldn't remember Mr. Saxe ever raising his voice. He was always kind to the orphans—teaching them how to do farm work without ever losing his patience.

"Are you going to follow the rules, or not?" Mr. Saxe said. "I'm waiting for an answer."

Another pause. Jacob walked down to the bottom of the stairs, inched along the hallway, and peeked into the dining room.

"Of course, I'll follow the rules," Mr. Greenblatt said. "Do you think I want to jeopardize everything we've planned and worked for?" His voice was rising in pitch. It reminded Jacob of the women in the market, yelling out their wares until they were hoarse. "Do you think I want to hurt these poor orphans?"

Now it was Mr. Saxe's turn to pause. "I sure hope not!" He lowered his voice. Jacob crept closer. "Now tell me the truth. From the very beginning, were you planning to bring the orphans to America, and not to Canada? Maybe to join the other Mezritshers in Detroit?" He sat down heavily on one of the chairs. It creaked with his weight. "Be honest. Were you going to use Canada as a way to bring the orphans to America?"

Jacob swallowed hard. *I don't want to go to America. I want to stay right here—in Georgetown, in Canada.*

Mr. Greenblatt held out his arms, palms up. "Well, maybe I did. At first." He shrugged. "But now I see that that was a mistake."

"Are you sure? Maybe you're just saying that so I won't suspect you." Mr. Saxe leaned forward and put his hands on his knees. "Or maybe, just maybe, you won't bring them all back here after the concert in New York!"

"Are you kidding? I'm planning no such thing!"

Mr. Saxe sighed. "I've tried to keep this farm school going for a long time." He brushed the hair off his forehead. "I've put a lot of time and energy—not to speak of most of my money—into this project. And my poor wife, Dora, she's working herself to death what with taking care of these kids…."

He stood up and began to pace the floor. "And if this concert doesn't raise enough money to keep the farm school going, then this whole project will go under."

Jacob crossed his arms and hugged his chest. *Dear God, I hope not!*

"Morris, don't worry so much," Mr. Greenblatt said. "Everything will be all right. Let's shake on it." He reached out his hand. Jacob almost smiled to see how Mr. Greenblatt had to stand on the tips of his toes just to reach Mr. Saxe's shoulder.

Mr. Saxe reluctantly shook Mr. Greenblatt's hand. "For all our sakes, I hope so."

Jacob heard the truck's horn beeping outside. He pressed himself against the wall, hoping the men wouldn't see him.

Jacob felt the tears welling up. *Will we stay on the farm? Or, will we have to leave this good place where I finally found a home? I want to stay here! Who knows if I'll ever be a real farmer or not? But for now, I want to stay.*

He shook his head and smiled to himself. *As if shaking my head is going to get rid of my worries.* He rushed out the door.

Chapter 31

The train chugged its way from Georgetown, stopping every quarter hour or so to pick up or drop off passengers or freight.

"Don't mind the 'milk run,'" Mr. Saxe said as he waved them good-bye. "Without it, I wouldn't be in business." Jacob could see he was making an effort to make a joke. "Good luck in New York. I know you'll make me and your teachers proud!"

The land they passed through was dotted here and there with melting piles of snow or muddy puddles. *This trip feels different than other trips*, Jacob thought. *We're leaving but this time, I know we'll come back.* He swallowed hard. *At least, I hope so.*

When they arrived at Toronto's new Union Station to change trains, Jacob marvelled at the marble arches at each end of the Grand Hall, the fancy metal tiles on the ceiling, and the huge clock in the center of the cavernous space.

He felt a shiver up and down his spine. *It's not like the train station in my nightmare*, he thought. *The lights are shining here. It's big and open.* He squared his shoulders. *Most of all, I'm with my friends now. I'm not alone.*

The group made its way to the train that would take them to New York City. They settled into the car that had been reserved for them. They began to play cards or checkers—Abe the Tall still beat everyone—to read a book or magazine, doze, or sing songs.

As Jacob gazed out the window, from time to time he saw children by the side of the tracks as they waved to the engineer. Soon, the city gave way to small towns or scattered farms. After a few hours, the train stopped in Niagara Falls, before crossing the border into the United States.

A man wearing a blue uniform and peaked cap slowly walked through the train and called, "Papers ready, please! Have your papers ready!"

Mr. Greenblatt handed their tickets and a letter to the man. "I think you'll find everything is in order." Mr. Greenblatt pointed to the piece of paper. "These young people are going to New York City to play at Carnegie Hall."

The man read the letter. The orphans had to stand up when he called their names. When he was finally finished, he handed the letter back to Mr. Greenblatt. "So, you're heading to New York City, are you?"

Is everything in order, the way Mr. Greenblatt kept telling us? Jacob wondered. *If not, will we be turned back?* He could feel his hands shaking but he tried to keep them still in his lap.

"We sure are!" Ezra said.

"That letter says you're to play in a mandolin concert at Carnegie Hall?"

"Yes, sir!" Abe the Tall said.

"I went to a concert there once a long time ago." The man had a dreamy look in his eyes. "It was grand, for sure." He paused. "Welcome to the United States. I wish you all the best of luck."

A chorus of "thank-yous" followed the man as he left the car.

Mr. Greenblatt stuffed the letter back into his briefcase, plopped down on his seat, and wiped his perspiring face with his handkerchief. "I'm glad we didn't have any trouble," he whispered to Mr. Podoliak, who was sitting beside him.

"Trouble? Why should we have trouble?"

After they had crossed the border, Mr. Greenblatt pulled out the lunch Mrs. Saxe had packed for everyone:

hard-boiled eggs, boiled potatoes, carrot sticks, pickles, cheese, Passover matzah (since it was Passover time), and apples.

Benjamin hit David gently on the head. "Because of you, we all have to eat matzah."

"There's going to be a trail of crumbs all the way from the train to Carnegie Hall," Abe the Tall added.

David shrugged. "So? Then we'll be able to find our way back to the station."

"That's what you think!" Benjamin said.

♫

As the train traveled through the tunnel under the Hudson River and approached Pennsylvania Station late that evening, Mr. Greenblatt stood up at the front of the car. "Children, make sure you have all your be-longings—suitcases, coats, hats, and—"

"—Mandolins!" Mr. Podoliak wagged his finger at Jacob.

They hurried out of the train and up the stairs.

Ezra whistled. "If we thought the station in Toronto was something, look at this one!"

Mr. Podoliak pushed his glasses up the bridge of his nose. "I read somewhere that the station in Toronto was modelled after this one."

"It's the grandest one in North America," Mr. Greenblatt said.

The children craned their necks to look at the metal latticework high up on the ceiling, the huge clock with its black Roman numerals that seemed to be suspended over the enormous hall, and the tall Greek columns that made Jacob feel small and insignificant.

After a few minutes, Mr. Greenblatt herded them past the granite pillars at the entrance to the station and into the hustle and bustle of the big city. Jacob felt as if a wall of noise and lights was crashing into him.

"Ezra," Jacob said, "when we were back in Mezritsh, did you ever think we'd see such a big city?"

"Gosh! Never!"

They followed Mr. Greenblatt to the subway entrance. "Now gather around me and listen," he shouted above the noise of honking cars and taxis moving along the busy thoroughfare.

"While you wait for the subway, don't stand close to the edge of the platform." He took a big breath. "When the subway comes, get on fast because the doors close quickly. Stay together as much as you can and—"

"Mr. Greenblatt," David said, "what if we get separated from the group?"

Mr. Greenblatt shook his head. "You'd better not, but if you do, get off at the Seventh Avenue stop."

"We'll count heads when we get off," Mr. Podoliak said.

Mr. Greenblatt stared at Mr. Podoliak, as if he resented being interrupted. "Three stops on the subway, back up to the street, then a short walk to our hotel." He held out his arms, as if trying to keep them all together; as if he were a worried shepherd and they were his straying sheep. "Remember! Only three stops!"

They followed Mr. Greenblatt down the steps and into the subway. When they entered the subway car, Benjamin yelled above the noise of the grinding wheels, "I love this subway! And it goes underground!"

"Do you think Toronto will ever get one?" David said.

"I doubt it," Abe the Tall said. "It must cost a fortune!"

When they reached their stop, Mr. Greenblatt led them back up to the street and directly to their hotel. "Two kids to a room," he said. "No arguing about who you'll be with." He called out their names and handed each of them their keys. "Freshen up and meet me in the lobby in half an hour." He smiled a weary smile. "We'll find a place to eat supper, and then it's early to bed."

"In the morning, come down here for breakfast at nine o'clock sharp," Mr. Podoliak said. "Then we go to the Hall for our dress rehearsal at ten."

"Carnegie Hall is waiting," Mr. Greenblatt said.

"That's what I'm afraid of," Jacob said.

Suddenly, something that had seemed only an impossible dream was now becoming a reality.

Epilogue

Carnegie Hall, New York City

April 8, 1928, 8 p.m.

As Jacob and the other members of the orchestra walked along the dim hallway to the backstage room, he could not see who or what were in the photos lined along the gray walls. He guessed they were photos of people who had performed here, from the time when Carnegie Hall had first been built in 1891. *So long ago!* he thought. *Were they as nervous as I am before they had to go on stage?*

"Go ahead, children," Mr. Greenblatt said. "I need to speak with Mr. Podoliak about something."

The children hurried into the room that was filling up with various people who would be performing in the concert along with the mandolin players. Some were putting on touches of lipstick and rouge; others were brushing or straightening their clothes; still others were warming their voices with scales or lip exercises. Others were tuning their instruments or practicing difficult parts of their music.

Jacob tried to brush the hair out of his eyes with one hand while holding onto his mandolin with the other. He gazed at the other members of the orchestra.

Ezra was whistling under his breath. Perla and Rose were whispering and giggling as usual. Benjamin was biting his fingernails. David was making sure his *kippah* was set firmly on his head. Abe the Tall was clenching his fists. Alex was looking a little pale.

Suddenly, Jacob had the urge to pee. He tapped an older man on the shoulder. In his best English, he said, "Please, sir, where is the...toilet?"

The man gestured behind Jacob. "Out the hall and to the right," he said. "Greenhorns," he muttered under his breath.

As Jacob made his way toward the washroom, he heard Mr. Greenblatt and Mr. Podoliak speaking in low voices.

"What do you mean?" Mr. Podoliak said. "What telegram?"

Jacob stopped in his tracks. He peeked around the corner.

Mr. Greenblatt waved a piece of paper in front of

Mr. Podoliak's face. "This telegram." He handed it to Mr. Podoliak, who peered at it through his thick glasses.

Mr. Podoliak handed the paper back to Mr. Greenblatt. "But...it can't be!" He took off his glasses and wiped his eyes. "He was just a boy!"

"I'm afraid it's true." Mr. Greenblatt sighed and put the telegram back into his jacket pocket. "The last I heard, Nathan had recovered and was up for adoption with a nice Jewish couple in Halifax." He breathed deeply. "But the sickness must have weakened him." His shoulders sagged. "Three days ago, he was taken to the hospital. Yesterday, he died."

Nathan died? Jacob felt like screaming and crying at the same time. *How could he die?*

Mr. Podoliak put his handkerchief back in his pocket. "What do we do now? Do we tell the children?"

Mr. Greenblatt shook his head. "I don't think so. It will just upset them." He took out his pocket watch. "And it's almost time to start."

Jacob hurried to the bathroom. *What should I do?* he thought as he washed his hands. *Maybe I should tell the others what I heard. When I didn't tell the grown-ups about Nathan, it only made things worse.* He dried his hands on the pull-down towel. *Maybe Nathan wouldn't have gotten so sick. Maybe it's not a good thing to keep secrets.*

On the other hand, maybe Mr. Greenblatt is right. It would only upset everyone, and this concert is important. He pressed his lips together. *Mr. Saxe said the future of the farm school depends on the money we raise here.*

Jacob straightened his back. *I'll tell the others afterwards.* He pushed the door open and made his way back down the hall. *As for me, I'll play the mandolin like I've never played before!*

Jacob walked up to Abe the Tall and tapped him on the shoulder.

"What do you want, squirt?" Abe the Tall said.

Jacob licked his dry lips. "I need to talk to everyone. It's important."

Abe the Tall put two fingers to his mouth and whistled loudly.

"What's wrong?" Benjamin said. "Sounds like you're calling the horses from the pasture!"

"Gather 'round, everyone," Abe the Tall said. "Jacob has something to tell you."

"Listen, everyone!" Jacob took a big breath. "Nathan can't be here with us today." He could feel the lump rise in his throat. "But let's play our music like we've never played before. And…let's dedicate this concert to Nathan."

Ezra made a thumbs-up gesture. "Good idea!"

"So, we'll do it?" Jacob said.

"We will!"

Just then, the stage manager entered the room. "Five minutes until curtain," he said. "Take your places please."

Everyone scrambled to get into line.

"The kids have gumption," Mr. Greenblatt said.

"What did you expect?" Mr. Podoliak said. "They've come a long way from where they began."

Jacob peeked at the gold velvet curtain that separated the performers from the audience. He imagined his life up to this point, as if the curtain were a screen and his life, the moving pictures. He closed his eyes. He remembered the people—some dead, some living—who had brought him to this place.

Mama and Papa, he and his sister Raisele—all living together in two rooms, in faraway Mezritsh. The influenza that had taken them from him. Uncle Isaac and Aunt Malka, who had taken him in, even when they had their own children to take care of. Mrs. Anna Adler, who had shown him kindness at the orphanage. Mr. Greenblatt, whose idea it was to bring the orphans to Canada. Mr. Podoliak, who had taught them that they could achieve anything they wanted if they only worked hard. Finally, Morris Saxe and his wife, who had welcomed the orphans to Canada and treated them like family.

Jacob thought he could also see a long line of people stretching into the future—a line of his children and grandchildren and those of the other orphans standing with him. He smiled to himself. *What will I be like? An old man with a beard?*

Now here they were at last, getting ready to walk out onto the stage of this great concert hall. *Please, God, please stop this wild fluttering in my stomach. Please let me do what I'm supposed to do.*

He closed his eyes and breathed deeply. The group stood silently, ready to mount the steps and go on stage. Jacob's heart beat so loudly that he was sure it could be heard all the way up to the last row of the balcony.

He clutched his mandolin tightly to his chest. He felt the warm wood spreading calm and comfort throughout his body.

"Are you all right?" Ezra asked. "You seem to be in another world."

"I'm okay. I was thinking about everything that brought us here."

Ezra put his arm around Jacob's shoulders. "Gosh darn! It's time to stop dreaming and time to make music." He peered at his friend. "Are you ready?"

Jacob inhaled deeply. He was ready.

HISTORICAL NOTES

MEZRITSH, POLAND

In the country of Poland in eastern Europe lies the town of Mezritsh (Międzyrzec Podlaski). Mezritsh is about sixty miles (100 kilometers) southeast of Warsaw. In the year 1927, when this story takes place, it would have taken about four hours to travel by train from Mezritsh to Warsaw, the capital of Poland.

When World War I ended in 1918, about 20,000 Jews lived in Mezritsh. They made up about eighty per cent of the town's population. Most worked in the brush-making industry, which exported products all over the world. Others were storekeepers or worked as tailors, shoemakers, or tanners.

The town's Jewish community had a savings-and-loan association, a free-loan fund, a soup kitchen, a

hospital, and an orphanage. The community boasted many educational institutions: Hebrew schools and Yiddish schools; Orthodox schools and secular schools; Zionist schools and Bundist schools. Several Yiddish newspapers were published in the town, and Jewish residents participated in numerous activities, like clubs, libraries, sports, drama associations, and even a brass band.

During World War II (1939–1945), Germans, uniformed police officers (the SCHUPO, short for *Schutzpolizei*), and the Polish "Blue Police" committed mass murders of Jews from Mezritsh and the surrounding communities, or sent Jews to the death camps of Treblinka and Majdanek. In August 1946, the Jewish population of Mezritsh amounted to only forty-seven people; most of them left the town in the following years. The last Jewish Holocaust survivor in Mezritsh died in 1997.

FOUNDING OF THE MEZRITSH ORPHANAGE

The building was purchased in 1920 by Moshe Gedalia Sajeta. He had emigrated from Mezritsh to New York City, and made his fortune in the shoe business.

In the *Mezritsh Yizkor Book*, former residents remember: "In 1920, immediately after the First World War, when many Jews in America felt a pull to see the towns from where they came, that pull also affected Moshe Sajeta. There was a great danger in traveling to Europe at that time, but Sajeta could not wait any longer. Through his own means, with nobody's help, he set out on a ship and traveled to Mezritsh....

"Arriving in Mezritsh, Moshe Gedalia immediately began to gather together the war orphans. He then purchased the known house at Czachowicz, and with some help from the Mezritshers in America, the first Jewish orphanage in Poland was opened in Mezritsh.... Later, Eliahu Greenblatt became involved in the project."

BIOGRAPHIES OF REAL PEOPLE MENTIONED IN *JACOB AND THE MANDOLIN ADVENTURE*

Anna Adler (d. 1943): Anna Adler was a highly respected member of the Mezritsh Jewish community. She helped found the first library and reading hall in the city; established the first Russian school in Mezritsh, and later, the first Yiddish school. During the 1920s, she became involved with the Jewish Orphanage (Children's Home), where she "imbued her heart and soul." It became "an exemplary institution under her supervision." After the death of her husband, Shepka Adler, she traveled to Leipzig and later to Paris. When World War II broke out, Adler escaped to southern France, where she went into hiding. On September 10, 1943, she was captured by the Gestapo. Before she could be taken in for questioning, and probably torture, she took poison and died.

Eli(ahu) Greenblatt: Originally from Mezritsh, Eli Greenblatt settled in Detroit, Michigan. His goal was to help Mezritsh Jewish orphans come to the United States. However, because of restrictive quotas in the U.S. after 1924, Greenblatt asked Morris Saxe to help bring the orphans to Canada. He brought two groups of orphans to Canada—the first in 1927; the second, in 1929. Unfortunately, the second group of orphans did not all fit the criteria set by the Canadian government. Some were not "full" orphans; others were not within the correct age range. Furthermore, Greenblatt was accused of accepting $400 per orphan to bring them to Canada. For these reasons, as well as economic hardships during the Depression, the Canadian Jewish Farm School collapsed in the early 1930s.

Pesach (Phillip) Podoliak (d. 1974): Pesach Podoliak was a music teacher in Mezritsh. Apparently, another teacher was supposed to accompany the first group of orphans to Canada in 1927, but because the man had an eye infection, Podoliak went instead. At that time, he was married to Helen (Chaia) and they had two daughters. His wife and children later joined him in

Morris Saxe, founder of the
Canadian Jewish Farm School.

Toronto. Podoliak was a musician, teacher, and composer in Toronto and also performed with the Shevchenko Mandolin Orchestra.

Morris Saxe (1878–1965): Born on a Jewish agricultural colony near Kiev, Ukraine, Morris Saxe was an adherent of the Jewish back-to-the-land movement. When Saxe arrived in Canada in 1902, he enrolled in the Ontario Agricultural College in Guelph. In 1907, he purchased his first farm. Three years later, Saxe opened a creamery in Acton, where he also owned a tannery, a knitting-needle firm, and Acton's first "moving-picture theatre." In 1917, Saxe moved with his family to Georgetown where he opened another business, the Georgetown Creamery.

After establishing a training school on his farm in 1926, Saxe agreed to bring a group of orphans to Georgetown. He once said, "Our plan here is to train them [young Jews] in English as well as modern agricultural methods. Then they would be able to get out and get a start for themselves and I am sure would make better citizens than many of those who go to the cities."

By bringing two groups of Jewish orphans from Mezritsh to Canada in 1927 and 1929, Morris Saxe most likely saved their lives. After World War II, he tried to bring a group of Jewish orphans, Holocaust

survivors, to Canada. In late October 1946, the Canadian Department of Immigration, headed by Mr. A.L. Joliffe, refused his request in spite of Saxe's having raised $30,000 with the support of many people from the Jewish community.

Morris Saxe married Dora (née Gerzog) in 1909. They had five children: Miriam (Mina), Pearl, David, Percy, and Leona. Dave Fleishman, who inspired this book, is Morris Saxe's grandson and creator of the film, *A Man of Conscience*.

THE MEZRITSH ORPHANS

For the rest of their lives, most of the orphans kept in touch with each other. The friendships they formed in the orphanage and at the Canadian Jewish Farm School made a lasting impression on them. One of the orphans once said, "I came to the farm in 1927…and it was very nice. I had a wonderful time. Mr. Saxe was so good to me, and Mrs. Saxe. I never had it in my life like I had on the farm."

Left, top: Dora Saxe (standing left) with a group of orphan girls.

Left, bottom: Group of boys eating a meal together outside at the Canadian Jewish Farm School in Georgetown, Ontario.

A group of children at the
Canadian Jewish Farm School.

The exterior of the dormitory building at
the Canadian Jewish Farm School.

Boys with calves.

A mandolin like Jacob might have played.

Carnegie Hall program, April 8, 1928.

Carnegie Hall in 1907.

Top: Traditional wooden houses in Międzyrzec (Mezritsh).
Bottom: Międzyrzec (Mezritsh) alley in the Old Town market.

SOURCES CONSULTED

BOOKS

(* Suitable for young people.)

———. *The Yad Vashem Encyclopedia of the Ghettos During the Holocaust*. Jerusalem: Yad Vashem, 2009.

*Baldwin, Douglas and Patricia. *Canadian Decades: 1920s*. Calgary: Weigl, 2012.

Brown, Ron. *The Last Stop: Ontario's Heritage Railway Stations*. Toronto: Polar Bear Press, 2002.

Coons, Lorraine and Alexander Varias. *Tourist Third Cabin: Steamship Travel in the Interwar Years*. New York: Palgrave Macmillan, 2003.

Cooper, Bruce Clement (ed.) *The Golden Age of Canadian Railways*. Stroud, Gloucestershire, UK: Worth Press, 2010.

Dawson, Philip and Bruce Peter. *Ship Style: Modernism and Modernity at Sea in the 20th Century*. London: Conway, 2010.

*Granfield, Linda. *Pier 21: Gateway of Hope*. Toronto: Tundra, 2000.

Horn, Yosef (ed.) *Mezritsh Yizkor Book*. Buenos Aires, Argentina: Assoc. of Former Residents of Mezritsh in Argentina, 1952. (Original title: *Mezritsh: zamlbukh in heylikn ondenk: fun di umgekumene Yidn.*)

Herald, Jacqueline. *Fashions of a Decade: The 1920s*. New York: Chelsea House, 2007.

Kyvig, David E. *Daily Life in the United States, 1920–1940: How Americans Lived Through the "Roaring Twenties" and the Great Depression*. Chicago: Ivan R. Dee, 2002.

*Lavery, Brian. *Ship: The Epic Story of Maritime Adventure*. New York: DK Publishing, 2004.

*Macauley, David. *Crossing on Time: Steam Engines, Fast Ships, and a Journey to the New World*. New York: Roaring Brook Press, 2019.

Maxtone-Graham, John. *Crossing & Cruising: From the Golden Era of Ocean Liners to the Luxury Cruise Ships of Today*. New York: Charles Scribner's Sons, 1992.

Mitic, Trudy Duivenvoorden and J.P. LeBlanc. *Pier 21: The Gateway that Changed Canada*. Halifax: Nimbus Publishing, 2011 (1988).

Okrent, Daniel. *The Guarded Gate: Bigotry, Eugenics, and the Law That Kept Two Generations of Jews, Italians, and other European Immigrants Out of America*. New York: Scribner, 2019.

*Renaud, Anne. *Pier 21: Stories from Near and Far* (Canadian Immigration Series). Montreal: Lobster Press, 2008.

Spalding, Simon. *Food at Sea: Shipboard Cuisine from Ancient to Modern Times*. London: Rowan & Littlefield, 2015.

Stanway, Paul. *Birth of a Nation: Canada in the 20th Century*. Edmonton: CanMedia, 2006.

Streissguth, Tom. *Eyewitness to History: The Roaring Twenties*. New York: Facts on File, 2001.

*Tames, Richard. *Picture History of the 20th Century: The 1920s*. Mankato, Minn.: Sea-to-Sea, 2006.

Turner, Gordon. *Empress of Britain: Canadian Pacific's Greatest Ship*. Toronto: Stoddart, 1992.

*Welldon, Christine. *Pier 21: Listen to My Story*. Halifax: Nimbus, 2012.

ARTICLES

Gladstone, Bill. "Morris Saxe and the Canadian Jewish Farm School." *The Canadian Jewish News*, June 10, 2015: https://www.cjnews.com/news/feature-morris-saxe-canadian-jewish-farm-school.

Lacasse, Simon-Pierre. 1. "Sionisme de gauche, agriculturalisme et immigration juive au Canada au lendemain de la Grande Guerre." *Canadian Jewish Studies / Études Juives Canadiennes*, vol. 24, 2016, 38–59.

Lipinsky, Jack. "Immigration Opportunity or Organizational Oxymoron? The Canadian Jewish Farm School and the Department of Immigration, 1925–46." *Canadian Jewish Studies / Etudes Juives Canadiennes*, vol. 21, 2013 [2014], 51–65.

FILMS, VIDEOS, WEBSITES

A Man of Conscience (documentary): https://www.youtube.com/watch?v=hlMwHr5jfKU. Produced by Cayle Chernin and David Fleishman. Directed by Cayle Chernin. 1997.

Canadian Jewish Archives: https://www.cjarchives.ca/en/

Canadian Museum of Immigration at Pier 21: https://pier21.ca

Miedzyrzec Podlaski (Mezritsh, Poland): http://shtetlroutes.eu/en/miedzyrzec-podlaski-przewodnik/

History of Mezritsh: http://www.mezritch.org.il/eng-text/eng-town.html

Ontario Jewish Archives: http://www.ontariojewisharchives.org/

Victoria Bridge, Montreal: https://www.youtube.com/watch?v=Q8keAEKDD6c

PHOTO CREDITS

Page 208: Ontario Jewish Archives, Blankenstein Family Heritage Centre, item 1675; page 210: Ontario Jewish Archives, Blankenstein Family Heritage Centre, item 1678 and item 1660; page 212: Ontario Jewish Archives, Blankenstein Family Heritage Centre, item 1661; page 213: Ontario Jewish Archives, Blankenstein Family Heritage Centre, item 3047 and item 1656; page 241: Mandolin © iStockphoto; page 216: Drewniane domy by Ireneusz S. Wierzejski is licensed under CC BY-SA 3.0 and Zaułek przy Rynku Starego Miasta by Ireneusz S. Wierzejski is licensed under CC BY-SA 3.0.

ACKNOWLEDGMENTS

Lisa Barrier, Digital Collections Associate, Carnegie Hall, New York City.

Donna Bernardo-Ceriz, Managing Director, Ontario Jewish Archives, Toronto.

Faye Blum and Michael Friesen, Archivists, Ontario Jewish Archives, Toronto.

Derek Boles, Chief Historian, Toronto Railway Historical Association.

Ina Cohen and Deborah Schranz, Librarians, Jewish Theological Seminary, New York.

Michael Cole and Sheila Smolkin, Archivists, Holy Blossom Temple, Toronto.

Steven Crainford, Royal Botanical Gardens, Burlington, Ontario.

Joseph Galron, Head, Hebraica and Jewish Studies, Ohio State University, Columbus, Ohio.

Avraham Groll, Director; Lance Ackerfeld, Coordinator; Rabbi Jamie Kotler, Coordinator, *Mezritsh Yizkor Book*, JewishGen.org.

Fruma Mohrer, Former Chief Archivist, YIVO Institute, New York.

Nina Pena, Librarian, Toronto Reference Library.

Memories about Morris Saxe, the orphans, and Georgetown: Michelle Baier, Harriet Etkin, Pearl Levy, Gert Rogers, Anne Freeman, Mark Kornheiser, Linda Stitt.

Dr. Jack Lipinsky, Department Head, Jewish History and Identity, Associated Hebrew Schools, Toronto, for reading a draft of this novel and offering very helpful suggestions.

Esther Podoliak, daughter of Mr. Pesach (Phillip) Podoliak, who was the orphans' music teacher.

Rona Arato, Sydell Waxman, Lynn Westerhout, Frieda Wishinsky: My writers' group—always there for me.

Lynn Westerhout and Anne Freeman, who lent their mandolins to me.

Toronto Public Library, for their Musical Lending Library (sponsored by Sun Life).

Ginger Kautto, for her patience with this very beginner mandolin player.

Sarah, Charlotte, and Bill, for their excellent tour of the *SS Keewatin*, Port McNicoll, Ontario.

Other people along the way:
- Meryl Arbing
- Shirley Baral
- Ruth Chernia
- Max and Julia Dublin
- Cecile Freeman
- Pam Halpern
- Rabbi Jordan Helfman, Holy Blossom Temple

- Bob Hodes
- Ed Levy, for generously sharing his knowledge of trains and stations
- Myrna Levy, for encouragement, ballet buddy, and numerous cups of tea
- Janna Nadler
- Kalina Serlin
- Paula Stitt, for her family poultry stuffing recipe
- Evan Turner
- Kalle Vaga, who shared with me his vast knowledge of trains, ships, and travel during the 1920s
- Sheryn Weber
- Judy Winberg

Dave Fleishman, who brought the story of his grandfather to my attention in the first place. Without his inspiration and support, this book would never have been written.

Last, but certainly not least, thanks go to my perceptive and kind editor, Gillian Rodgerson, as well as the wonderful people at Second Story Press: Margie Wolfe, Melissa Kaita, Emma Rodgers, Phuong Truong, Yasmine Lee, Jordan Ryder, Michaela Stephen, and Barbara Howson.

ABOUT THE AUTHOR

Anne Dublin is an award-winning writer of historical novels and biographies for young people. Her historical novels include *The Orphan Rescue*, *44 Hours or Strike!*, and *A Cage Without Bars*. Anne has also written several biographies: *June Callwood: A Life of Action*, *Bobbie Rosenfeld: The Olympian Who Could Do Everything*, and *Dynamic Women Dancers*. Anne lives in Toronto.